Wishlist Beyond the Stars

Abhay Chaudhary

Published by Notion Press

Cover Design by Abhay Chaudhary

Printed in India

For inquiries, please contact:

[abhaychaudhary1605@gmail.com]

[Connect on Instagram: abhay.chaudhary.18]

Dedication

To my family, whose unwavering support and love have been my guiding stars. Your belief in my dreams has made this journey possible.

Epigraph

"In the vast cosmic dance, dreams take flight,

Where wishes weave with stars in the night.

Through trials and turns, our hearts ignite,

In the cosmic ballet, our spirits alight."

— Abhay Chaudhary

Author's Note

Dear Readers,

As I embark on the thrilling journey of introducing you to "Wishlist Beyond the Stars," my heart swells with excitement and gratitude. My name is Abhay Chaudhary, and this book is not just a creation; it's a piece of my soul woven into the fabric of words.

In a world often clouded by uncertainties, I embarked on this literary odyssey with a singular purpose - to showcase that amidst the chaos, goodness still thrives. This marks my maiden venture into the realm of fiction, a journey I undertook with unwavering dedication, pouring my heart and soul into every sentence.

The characters you'll meet in these pages—Dushyant, the culinary maestro; Khwaaish, the YouTube sensation and poet; and Mannat, navigating the corporate world—are not just figments of imagination; they are living, breathing entities in my mind, brought to life by the strokes of my pen.

As I penned down their stories, I aimed to breathe life into each character, making them as real to you as they are to me. "Wishlist Beyond the Stars" isn't just a narrative; it's a cosmic dance of dreams, love, and friendship set against the vast backdrop of the universe.

The story revolves around Dushyant, a chef with a passion for poetry, and his journey to connect with Khwaaish, a YouTube sensation whose words resonate with his soul. The universe unfolds their love story, guided by the steadfast presence of Mannat, a friend determined to transform their Wishlist into a constellation of realized dreams.

This book is an exploration of the magical intersection of dreams and reality, where wishes dance with the stars, defying the limitations of the earthly realm. Each chapter contributes its essence to the cosmic tapestry, unraveling a celestial magic that will captivate your imagination.

As you turn the pages, I invite you to join us on this celestial odyssey. Let the wishes beyond the stars resonate with your own dreams, and may the cosmic ballet within these pages enchant and inspire you.

Thank you for being a part of this cosmic adventure. Your journey through "Wishlist Beyond the Stars" is about to begin, and I am thrilled to have you by my side.

With celestial anticipation,

Abhay Chaudhary

Introduction

Step into the captivating universe of "Wishlist Beyond the Stars," where the story revolved around three central characters—Dushyant, the culinary maestro; Khwaaish, a YouTube sensation and poet; and Mannat, Dushyant's close friend navigating the corporate world.

Met Dushyant, a chef with a deep love for poetry and playing the guitar, who shared his thoughts and dreams with Mannat, his best friend from a renowned company. In moments of solace, Dushyant immersed himself in poetry and books, often tuning in to YouTube for inspiration. One day, he stumbled upon Khwaaish's poetry, and it resonated with him deeply. Determined to know more, he embarked on a challenging journey to approach Khwaaish, a renowned figure with a massive fan following.

As Dushyant found a unique way to connect with Khwaaish, their encounters led to dates, love, and eventually a decision to embark on the sacred journey of marriage. United by their dreams, they created a Wishlist, pledging to fulfill eleven wishes together. While Khwaaish and Dushyant managed to manifest a few wishes, life took an unexpected turn, disrupting the harmony of their existence. The universe, with its mysterious ways, set forth challenges that seemed insurmountable.

In this cosmic dance, Mannat emerged as a steadfast friend, striving to transform their Wishlist into a constellation of realized wishes. The narrative unfolded across six captivating chapters, each contributing its essence and unique story to the cosmic tapestry.

The universe played its own game, and the characters grappled with unforeseen twists and turns. "Wishlist Beyond the Stars" invite readers to explore a world where dreams defied reality, love transcended boundaries, and friendships became guiding stars in the vast cosmic canvas.

Did the Wishlist manifest against the backdrop of the universe's whims, or did the cosmic ballet lead to unforeseen destinations? Readers join us on this celestial odyssey, where every chapter unveiled a new facet of life's wishes beyond the stars. As you turn the pages, you're enchant by the celestial magic woven into the narrative, beckoning into a world where wishes danced with the stars.

Table of Contents:

Chapter 1- Whispers of Love

In a serene corner of New Delhi, where the scent of spices wafted through the air, lived Dushyant, a young and skillful chef. His culinary prowess transformed ingredients into delightful symphonies of flavor, pleasing the palates of those fortunate enough to savor his creations. Yet, beneath the bustling kitchen and aromatic dishes, his heart yearned for a deeper connection—a longing for love that whispered softly in the background of his life.

Dushyant, with his wavy hair and a colorful apron marked by his cooking adventures, skillfully moved through the busy restaurant life. Each day brought the sizzling sounds of pans, the clatter of cutlery, and the constant activity in the kitchen. Amidst this lively chaos, his mind often wandered to dreams beyond the hot pots and grilling sounds.

Dushyant doesn't just envision his future within the busy confines of his restaurant kitchen. His dreams soar higher, aiming to establish his own cloud kitchen. In this space, his culinary creations won't be limited by the usual restaurant setup. With careful saving and detailed planning, every rupee he sets aside brings him a step closer to transforming his culinary aspirations into a tangible reality.

Away from the noisy kitchen filled with the sounds of clanking pots and pans, Dushyant discovers a sense of calm in the soft strumming of his guitar and the beautifully woven verses of poetry that touch the depths of his soul. His fondness for music and poetry goes beyond being just a way to pass the time; it serves as a profound wellspring of inspiration. This inspiration, drawn from the melodies and poetic words, infuses distinctive and special flavors not only into his dishes but also into the tapestry of his everyday life.

Dushyant was picky about his friends, preferring a small but close-knit circle. Mannat, his best friend since college, was a crucial part of this inner circle. Despite her busy job at a famous company, Mannat and Dushyant shared everything with each other. Whether it was celebrating successes, tackling challenges, or discussing dreams, they confided in one another. Their friendship was like a safe haven where every detail of life, no matter how big or small, was valued and treasured.

Dushyant's relationships with his parents have made him a bit careful about making new friends. The problems at home have had a strong effect on him, making it tough for him to believe in people quickly. The constant troubles in his family have left deep marks on Dushyant, making him approach relationships with caution. Still, in the midst of all these difficulties, he finds comfort in a small group of friends who have been with him through thick and thin. This special friendship gives him a sense of peace and support, helping him feel secure in the face of life's uncertainties.

Dushyant and Mannat's friendship is not limited to the regular ways people usually talk. In the world of social media, they show how much they enjoy each other's company by sharing fun videos, telling amusing stories, and giving a peek into their everyday lives. Their online conversations are like a vibrant display of a friendship that's built on laughter and happy moments, overcoming any distance that might separate them physically. Through the colorful collection of their online talks, they make their friendship stronger, turning even the digital space into a place where they can share and enjoy experiences together.

Mannat, who always lively and full of energy, often became the one who shared stories in their online escapades. She really loved to talk, and sometimes she talked a lot, but Dushyant really liked the lively conversations that happened. In the beautiful melody of their friendship, Mannat's constant chatting added a lively tune, making regular moments turn into colorful and treasured memories that they both really appreciated.

The link between Dushyant and Mannat was more than just on the computer or phone; it even affected the choices Mannat made in her personal life. When she thought about getting into a romantic relationship, it was really important for her to get Dushyant's approval. It wasn't just something she did routinely; what he thought mattered a lot. It showed a strong foundation of trust and understanding, highlighting the deep nature of their bond. Despite the various experiences in life, their friendship was like a solid support, where moments of shared laughter and online adventures were like the threads weaving together the fabric of their lasting connection.

Their Backstory, how Dushyant and Mannat met.

"Dushyant's initial experience on his first day of college, he entered with confidence and ease, as if he belonged there. However, upon entering, Dushyant realized that there were no available seats. This caused him to panic, and he started searching for a place to sit. Eventually, he noticed an empty seat next to Mannat. Initially, Dushyant had a preconceived notion about Mannat, thinking, "She must be super fancy and probably doesn't talk to guys." This indicates that he assumed Mannat might be a bit reserved or not interested in talking to male

classmates. However, before Dushyant could gather the courage to introduce himself, Mannat took the initiative and introduced herself first.

"Hey! I'm Mannat. It's my first day, and I'm so nervous about potential ragging. I don't know anyone here. Can you please hang out with me today? If I have a guy with me, maybe the seniors won't rag me. Please?" Dushyant chuckled and agreed, "Sure, I'm Dushyant, introduced himself, It's my first day too."

From there, Mannat unleashed a flood of stories—school life, love stories, breakups—no holds barred. Dushyant couldn't help but wonder if this was her regular talkative self or just the excitement of the first day. He asked, "Do you always talk this much, or is today a special occasion?" She replied, "This is just who I am. Now, tell me, do you always talk so little, or is there a special reason today?"

Dushyant, a bit taken aback, responded, "Well, if you give me a chance to speak, I might have something to say." Mannat apologized, "Oops, sorry! Okay, tell me about yourself." Dushyant shared his story, but Mannat, being her bubbly self, kept interrupting with her tales. Dushyant quipped, "Am I going to have to endure this chatter throughout college?" She grinned, "Well, you're lucky to have me as a friend on first day. Life will be so much more fun with a buddy like me."

Dushyant, finding humor in the situation, said, "Alright then, today I declare you my first college friend, and I'm sticking with you for the rest of college life." Mannat, half-jokingly, declared, "I can't believe someone actually agrees to put up with my nonsense. If you believe in it, treat in the college canteen is a must." Dushyant smiled and said, "Deal, boss!"

Their friendship deepened during their college days, and even after all these years, they remain the best of friends."

Now, when Mannat discovered someone, she wanted to spend her life with, Dushyant couldn't help but feel a bit uncertain about this person who had become so crucial to her as she had a habit of trusting people easily. He talked to Mannat about his worries, carefully expressing his thoughts. He wanted her to be careful because he understood that decisions like these could have a big impact on her whole life. Even though he had his concerns, Dushyant respected Mannat's ability to make her own decisions. In the end, he gave his approval, telling her to follow her heart and make choices that felt right for her.

As Mannat entered this new chapter in her life, their friendship underwent some changes. The frequent conversations they used to have become less frequent, mainly because Mannat had more responsibilities and duties toward her soon-to-be husband. On Dushyant's side, he found comfort in different things. He immersed himself in the captivating world of storytelling, lost himself in the rhythmic tunes of his guitar, and discovered solace in the profound words of poetry. His work also became a safe place where he could focus his attention and creativity. This shift in their connection showed how their friendship was adapting as both of them navigated their own separate journeys.

Even though they didn't talk as much, the importance of Dushyant and Mannat's friendship didn't diminish; it kind of turned into this silent agreement. Mannat was busy building her new life, and during this time, Dushyant found his own place in the worlds of art and cooking. The strong connection between them, even though it was stretched a bit, stayed resilient, weaving through the stories of their separate journeys. Despite being far apart, their bond held on, influencing their own paths and stories in special yet connected ways.

One day, as Dushyant was exploring the big world of YouTube, he stumbled upon an incredibly interesting video. On this online space, a delightful girl appeared, acting as a storyteller, weaving a beautiful story using the soft hues of poetry. Her words were really genuine, unfolding the complexities of her past—a story tangled with the challenges of a relationship that didn't quite work out. The video painted a clear picture of her experiences, and Dushyant was completely engrossed in the emotional journey she conveyed through her storytelling.

The girl's story unfolded like a poignant melody, describing the lingering echoes of a love that faded away because of a heavy burden of indifference. Her partner, while not unfaithful, began to take her presence for granted, only offering small signs of affection despite the immense love she showered upon him. In a relationship where she poured her heart and soul, he responded with just a small fraction, knowing well that she, in her unwavering commitment, would never turn away. The story painted a vivid picture of the uneven balance in their relationship, with her dedication overshadowing his seemingly limited investment in their connection.

In every word of her story, she carefully picked each one, delivering them with a gentle touch, painting a clear picture of a love that wasn't reciprocated. Not only did she invest time and effort, but she poured her very soul into the relationship, only to find that her sincere efforts were met with a cold indifference that hurt even more than if there had been outright betrayal. It was a tale full of heartache, unmet expectations, and the silent pain of a love that struggled in the shadows of neglect. The story unfolded like a heartfelt expression of the emotional toll taken by a relationship where her deep commitments were met with a lack of care in return.

She recited the below poem-

In the quiet corridors of her heart, a symphony of pain,

Echoes of love unmet, like a gentle autumn rain.

She wove a tapestry of devotion, threads of care,

Yet, received in return, a vacant, cold air.

Her love, a garden tended with utmost grace,

But his gestures, mere shadows in the sacred space.

In the moonlit dance, where two souls should sway,

She found herself alone, in the absence of his ray.

A needle of longing, she threaded through the night,

But he remained oblivious, in the absence of her light.

A love that whispered promises, yet shattered like glass,

In the mosaic of heartache, where shattered dreams amass.

He took her for granted, a silent, painful decree,

Each teardrop a testament to what could never be.

In the gallery of her sorrow, a portrait painted in despair,

Love's requiem composed in the quietude of her prayer.

Her heart, a fragile vessel, sailed stormy seas,

Weathering the tempest, yet yearning for ease.

In the ballad of her pain, a haunting refrain,

A melody of love lost, dancing in the shadows of the arcane.

(The above poem portrays the emotional struggles of a woman who, despite investing deep care and devotion in her love, experiences unmet affection and gestures of indifference from her partner, leading to a poignant narrative of longing, heartache, and shattered dreams as she navigates the stormy seas of a one-sided relationship, ultimately finding solace in the haunting refrain of a love lost.)

As Dushyant immersed himself in the unfolding story, he felt a profound understanding stirring within him. The girl's poetic storytelling had this remarkable ability to go beyond the screen, reaching deep into the core of his own emotions and experiences, especially those entangled with his parents. Without realizing it at that moment, this unexpected encounter with her narrative became a meaningful event, marking the beginning of a connection that would shape and influence the upcoming chapters of his own personal story. Little did he know the significance of this chance meeting with her tale and the impact it would have on the unfolding narrative of his life.

In the gentle glow of his computer or phone screen, Dushyant stumbled upon a fascinating world within Khwaaish's YouTube channel. In this digital space, she unraveled stories and shared poetry, captivating him with her expressive way of telling tales. The name "Khwaaish" seemed to carry echoes of unfulfilled dreams and desires. Through her carefully chosen words, she revealed a deep understanding of love, and it was clear that she hadn't yet found someone worthy of her sincere affection. Dushyant found himself captivated by the charm of her narratives, each one holding a unique quality that stirred both his emotions and thoughts.

As he continued to watch her videos every day, he noticed a change happening within himself. A subtle admiration as his Crush started to grow, driven by the enchanting way she shared her thoughts and stories. Encouraged by this budding connection, he took a modest step and decided to follow her on Instagram. Aware that he was just one of many in her sizable group of followers, he found solace in quietly enjoying and appreciating her posts and stories without seeking attention or recognition. This silent admiration became a gentle thread weaving its way through his daily routine, adding a touch of warmth to his connection with Khwaaish's online presence.

Wanting to share his admiration, Dushyant occasionally sent direct messages to Khwaaish. In these messages, he poured his thoughts and feelings, hoping she would take notice. However, given her widespread popularity, he wasn't shocked that his messages went unnoticed, akin to throwing notes into a vast digital sea where they seemed to disappear without a trace. Despite the lack of acknowledgment, he continued to appreciate her content from afar, finding a quiet joy in being part of her online community.

Even though they didn't have direct conversations, he continued to relish her videos, creating a snug little corner in his digital world solely for savoring her content. He genuinely enjoyed the stories she shared, realizing that in the vast online realm, he was like a tiny dot, quietly finding joy and admiration from a distance. Despite the absence of direct interaction, he found comfort and happiness in being a silent admirer, content with the simple act of appreciating Khwaaish's work from the sidelines of the expansive internet space.

One day, as Dushyant was casually scrolling through Khwaaish's Instagram, he stumbled upon a post that sparked immense excitement within him. To his delight, she announced a live performance scheduled in Delhi for the upcoming Saturday. Without any second thoughts, he swiftly booked tickets, feeling a bubbling eagerness and thrill at the prospect of seeing the enchanting soul he admired behind the camera. He firmly believed that her beauty and talent would shine just as brightly in person, and the anticipation of experiencing her live performance added an extra layer of excitement to his plans. The idea of witnessing Khwaaish's artistry unfold in real-time filled him with joy and anticipation.

On the much-anticipated Saturday, Dushyant couldn't contain his excitement as he eagerly headed to the venue. A mix of anticipation and joy bubbled up inside him. Once seated, he fixed his gaze on the stage, eagerly awaiting the moment when she would step into the spotlight. The atmosphere in the venue buzzed with excitement as everyone in the audience shared the same eager anticipation for the upcoming performance. The air seemed to be filled with an electric energy, creating a tangible feeling of excitement that heightened the thrill of the moment. It was as if the entire place was pulsating with the collective anticipation of witnessing Khwaaish's live artistry unfold.

At last, the long-awaited moment arrived. When she stepped onto the stage, a hushed stillness settled over the crowd. He couldn't take his eyes off her, feeling captivated as if he had stumbled upon something truly magical. The words she shared weren't just poetry; they unfolded like a beautiful melody that reached deep into the heart. Every word, every verse she uttered seemed to pierce the soul, leaving a lasting and unforgettable impression on everyone lucky enough to be in the audience that day. It was like her words had a magical quality, creating an atmosphere that was both enchanting and emotionally resonant.

In that magical moment, Dushyant found himself captivated not just by Khwaaish's outer charm but also by the sheer brilliance of her inner spirit. Her words acted like a comforting balm to his longing heart, and as he listened, it felt as if he was witnessing the performance of a soulful angel. The connection that initially began in the digital world now flourished into a shared experience, where her words reached directly into the depths of his being, forming a deep and meaningful connection. It was as if her words had the power to touch his soul, creating a bond that went beyond the surface and resonated with the very core of his existence.

Here is the poetry beautifully recited by her:

In Granny's tales from way back when,

A love story that's sweet, like a gentle pen.

A Prince Charming, so kind and true,

Mending wounds and love that grew.

In storybooks, the dreams unfold,

A love so precious, a tale retold.

But as we grow, doubts may bloom,

Is this love real, or just a room?

Granny smiles, her eyes so wise,

"Such love exists," she softly implies.

Yet skepticism lingers in the air,

Do these prince(s) exist out there?

The girl, now grown, holds on to doubt,

In books, these loves play out.

Reality whispers, "Can it be?"

Or just tales of fantasy?

Granny insists, a truth to share,

A love so real, beyond compare.

Yet many think it's just in books,

Not in life's varied looks.

So, the girl ponders, dreams in her heart,

A love that's real, a work of art.

In stories or life, where does it roam?

A mythical love or one to call home.

Granny's wisdom, a guiding light,

In books or life, love takes flight.

A tale spun in reality's embrace,

Where love finds its own grace.

(The poem captures the essence of a story passed down from Granny in her childhood, portraying an idealized love symbolized by a Prince Charming. This mythical love is depicted in storybooks, where the prince mends wounds and deeply treasures love. Despite skepticism about such extraordinary love existing in reality, Granny confirms its presence. The speaker acknowledges that many, including herself, tend to believe that such men only exist in books and stories, not in real life. The poem evokes a sense of nostalgia and explores the delicate balance between the romanticized ideals of fairy tales and the complexities of real-world romance, leaving room for contemplation on the nature of love.)

The poetry she shared resonated deeply with Dushyant, making him want to let her know that guys who appreciate by her Granny truly exist. Inspired by an idea, he quickly grabbed a piece of paper and a pen. With a touch of humor, he penned down a note expressing his feelings. In the note, he also included a short poem along with his contact number, hoping to convey his admiration for her in a lighthearted and creative way.

Hey Khwaaish, in the tales your Granny told,

Spinning charm under skies so bold.

Not a prince from books, but real and true,

I'm your fan, you're my crush, feeling a bit like a debut.

Beyond fairy tales, in life's real song,

I'm not just any prince; humor's where I belong.

A chance for laughs, love that'll stick around,

Drop me a message, let's turn this tale upside down.

Imagine a romance like a comic scene,

Where laughter rules, and love is the queen.

Not the usual prince, if you catch my drift,

Give it a shot, let's make this love lift.

In this comedy of hearts, let's steal the show,

A chance for love to bloom and grow.

I'm not your average prince, as you may know,

Contact me, and let's make this laughter flow!

(The poem is a light-hearted and humorous expression of affection from him to Khwaaish. It plays on the idea of traditional fairy-tale prince(s) by presenting a unique, real, and funny version of a prince. The writer (Dushyant), who has a crush on Khwaaish, introduces himself as a fan and suggests a love story that breaks away from conventional fairy tales. The poem emphasizes humor and a non-traditional perspective on romance, inviting her to consider a fun and laughter-filled relationship outside the usual expectations associated with fairy-tale princes.)

With utmost care, Dushyant handed over the note adorned with the poem to the person organizing the event. He leaned in and whispered, "Could you please give this to Khwaaish and let her know it's from her family? He wrote 'Emergency Occurred' on the front side of the note." The organizer, intrigued by the mysterious request, accepted the note with a nod.

As she received the note, a spark of curiosity lit up her eyes. The words "Emergency Occurred" on the front caught her attention, stirring a sense of intrigue. Wondering what urgent message awaited her, she unfolded the note and began reading the contents—the beautifully crafted poem expressing admiration. Completely unaware of the humorous surprise that awaited her in the message.

Watching her burst into laughter, Dushyant observed Khwaaish carefully tucking the note into her pocket. As the countdown to the event continued, the hours passed by slowly. After patiently waiting for what felt like five or six hours, a notification chimed on his phone. To his surprise, it was a WhatsApp message. The text read, "Hey there, Mr. Prince Charming. I got your note; thanks for being a fan. But guess what? I'm your Crush! Didn't see that one coming. What should I call you? Do you have a name, or should I just stick with Prince?" The unexpected message brought a delightful surprise, and Dushyant couldn't help but smile at the playful turn of events. It seemed like she had not only appreciated his note but also responded with a charming sense of humor.

Responding with a playful spirit, Dushyant chimed in, "Absolutely, you can call me the 'Prince'. How about giving me the green light to call you the Princess in return?" Adding a touch of humor, he continued the lighthearted banter, making the interaction feel like a whimsical exchange of titles in their newfound digital connection.

Her laughter echoed through their messages, creating a warm and jovial atmosphere. Seizing the opportune moment,

Dushyant decided to share his name. "I'm Dushyant," he revealed with a friendly tone. "I'm a chef, someone skilled not only at crafting delicious food but also at weaving interesting stories. What do you think about the idea of us joining forces to create some delightful tales together?"

She responded with a playful tone, saying, "Alright, 'Prince Chef,' take it easy. I'm an independent Storyteller, you know; I write my own tales." Unfazed, Dushyant persisted, replying, "How about we create our stories together? Let's start with a tale about a date. What do you think about that?"

She mentioned that she needed time to consider the idea and would let him know, mentioning her busy schedule with two upcoming shows. Worried about the possibility of not hearing from her, he admitted, "But I'm afraid you won't reply to my texts." She reassured him with a smile, saying, "Don't worry. If I don't feel like talking, I won't text you. Stay positive."

Feeling overjoyed and in a celebratory mood from their chat, another message appeared. It said, "Just making sure, do you also live in Delhi?"

He confirmed with excitement, saying, "Absolutely, I've been a Delhiite since the day I was born." In reply, she sent a laughing emoji and teasingly said, "Hold on for my message, Mr. Chef."

A few days after the cheerful chat with her, Dushyant caught up with Mannat and spilled the entire story. In response, Mannat gleefully shared that her boyfriend had proposed to her, and she was over the moon with happiness. Thrilled by each other's positive news, they decided to celebrate these exciting developments by throwing a party for one another. The air was filled with genuine joy as they expressed their happiness and excitement for the wonderful turns their lives were taking.

After a gap of two days, Mannat and Dushyant met. As they greeted each other with a warm hug, congratulations flowed between them. Mannat, with a playful smile, said to Dushyant, "Oh no, now my friend is going to be far away, how will I survive without you, Noddy?" Dushyant chuckled and replied, "Come on, we haven't even met yet, why are you thinking so far ahead?" Mannat teased him, saying, "I trust you to impress her; I have a feeling that finally, Prince finds his Cinderella." Blushing, Dushyant endured her playful teasing.

Curious about Mannat's boyfriend, Dushyant asked, "tell me, how did he propose? Is he treating you well?" Mannat happily replied, "I'm having a great time in this phase of life. We're both so happy for each other; may the evil eye stay away from us." They both raised a cheer in celebration of the happiness in their lives. The camaraderie between Mannat and Dushyant was evident in their banter and shared joy, making the moment even more special.

Chapter 2- Promises and Wishlist

Engrossed in his kitchen duties, Dushyant was interrupted by a notification.

"What's up, Mr. Chef?" read the message.

She continued, "I promised to text you, and here I am. I've decided to taste some food from a chef; I'm tired of local vendors. So, what's your specialty in cooking?"

Unable to resist the excitement after receiving her text, Dushyant impulsively decided to give her a call. To his surprise, she picked up, and like a parrot on speed dial, he rapidly listed off his entire menu. When she casually mentioned, "A coffee will work," his joy knew no bounds. The transition from her digital presence to the lively audio of her voice was enchanting for Dushyant. Lost in his own world, she curiously asked, "What happened?" Chuckling, he replied, "Nothing, just really in the mood for coffee?"

Her response was affirmative, "Yes, for coffee. Can we meet this Saturday at Connaught Place at Char Bar cafe at 5 pm?"

After eagerly counting down three days, Saturday finally dawned. Dushyant took special care in choosing his favorite outfit – grey jeans, a black shirt, and stylish Nike sneakers. When she arrived, they embraced warmly, and she exclaimed, "Mr. Chef, what a coincidence! We're twinning; I also chose grey jeans and a black top today." Interrupting with a smile, Dushyant added, "There's one more coincidence between us.

You have a tattoo of a half-moon on your finger, and I was born with a half-moon on my palm." She responded with an impressed, "Oh, you noticed my tattoo! That's amazing."

She said interesting tell me more about this half-moon story. He replied that "a half moon on the palm may symbolize a touch of mystique, creative romance, and a heightened sensitivity to emotions and physical connection. It suggests a unique, almost mystical, bond in romantic relationships".

"Wow, it means you have a romantic nature," she remarked. Dushyant responded with a playful tone, "Yes, you can try and experience it for yourself." A smile lit up her face as she expressed, "I think I find you interesting and cute." The atmosphere was light and filled with a sense of discovery as they exchanged compliments, hinting at a budding connection between them.

They spent a delightful 2-3 hours together, sharing their likes and dislikes, discussing their goals and aspirations. She revealed that she's currently working a job but plans to leave soon to pursue her shows full-time. He, in turn, expressed his dream of opening his own cloud kitchen. The conversation flowed seamlessly, touching on various interesting topics, including their travel experiences and more. He suddenly expressed, "I've written something for you. If you allow, can I share it?" She eagerly replied, "Yes, please do."

You resemble a rose, a dream to acquire,

The answer to the question I've sought, you inspire.

In your presence, a response I desire,

Like a quest fulfilled, you set my heart on fire.

(This poem is like comparing her to a beautiful rose. It's saying you're like a dream that I want to make mine. You are the answer to the questions I've been searching for, and being around you makes me want a response like when you fulfill a quest or find something I've been looking for. Your presence makes my heart feel like it's on fire, but in a good way, like something exciting and wonderful.)

Blushing, she responded, "Well, I am a poet and poem teller. How is it that you write so well?"

He replied, "I may prepare, but you're a born writer. I know you can create any poem instantly." She teased him, saying, "Oh, buttering." They both shared a laugh, and then she added, "Okay, by seeing this environment, I can make something." He agreed with a simple "Okay."

Today, the weather speaks a tale,

A meeting with a pure-hearted lad, without fail.

Such scenes arrive once in a while,

As we witness this day, where does it take us, worthwhile?

(This little poem is talking about the weather today, saying it tells a story. It's about meeting a good-hearted person, and such moments happen only occasionally. She wonders where this day will take them and if it will be something meaningful or valuable. It's like the weather is creating a special moment, and she is curious about where it will lead.)

Blushing, he remarked, "So, this means it's a green signal. I'm hoping to see you again; our story cannot end here." She replied with sincerity, "I'm considering it, but trust me, today you made me feel alive. You made me believe in my Granny's words — guys like those in books and stories do exist."

She bought a book from the cafe's bookstore called "Forty Rules of Love." Dushyant noticed and said, "That's a fantastic book choice. I've read it before, and it's all about pure love. I believe we share a lot in common."

She exclaimed, "Wow! First, a chef, you do poetry, a reader, and what else is hidden in this personality?"

He laughed and said, "Soon, you'll come to know." She replied with a smile, "Okay, I will wait."

After exchanging goodbye hugs, she booked her cab to her house. They waved at each other, a silent promise of more meetings to come.

When she reached home, he asked her how she felt about the day, and she expressed that she liked it her poetic way.

Today was a blessing from above,

A stranger, a bit closer to my heart, the dove.

In him, there seemed to be a divine grace,

Grandma's words held truth, a belief to embrace.

The most significant realization was in self,

A Prince Chef's hospitality, like a magical spell.

He turned Cinderella into a princess, so divine,

A day of enchantment, where dreams entwine."

(The poem expresses gratitude for a blessed day, highlighting a newfound connection with a stranger who holds a special place in the writer's heart. There's a sense of divine grace and transformation, possibly influenced by the hospitality of a "Prince Chef." The day is described as enchanting, turning ordinary moments into something magical and extraordinary, echoing the theme of dreams intertwining with reality.)

Feeling a strong connection after their meeting, he decided to express himself through a voice note. In the note, he said, "Close your eyes and just listen." The audio he sent was a guitar version of the famous Titanic song "My Heart Will Go On." Through this musical gesture, he aimed to convey his emotions and share a beautiful melody that resonated with the depth of his feelings.

She was in utter shock and exclaimed, "You can play the guitar too?" He confidently replied, "Yes! Remember the half-moon on the palm? Rare, creative, and filled with love."

She replied, "Wow, you have magical hands, Chef-cooking food, playing guitar, writing. Really impressed." He teased, "There's more to come, just wait and relax, Selenophile."

With brimming excitement, he eagerly shared the details of his first date with Mannat, who responded with genuine joy for him. However, amidst the cheerful conversation, Mannat dropped a surprising bomb – she's getting engaged in a month. Playfully, she insisted, "You better come, and bring Khwaaish too. I want to meet her and tease you. I'll do my best to make her start hating you." Chuckling, he replied, "I can't promise that in just one meeting, but I'll give it a shot." Mannat added with a playful tone, "You have a month to figure it out. Remember the good old college days when you'd cram a 6-month semester in one night?" The exchange was filled with laughter and a sense of nostalgia. She used to continue telling him a story about herself, and he would patiently listen. He knew that as long as Mannat didn't finish her tale and disclose all the details, she wouldn't be able to sleep. He understood that Mannat liked to share every detail, and he was always willing to listen attentively until she felt satisfied. Their friendship was built on this understanding, where he respected her need to express herself fully, even if it meant a longer conversation.

After a three day-He texted To Khwaaish.

Dushyant: "Hey, Tale Teller! What's up? How are you doing?"

Khwaaish: "Wow, cute name! Just spinning tales and weaving dreams. What about you?"

Dushyant: "If you were a vegetable, you'd be a cute-cumber!"

Khwaaish: "Oh, please! That's the oldest one in the book. Try again, Chef Jokester!"

Dushyant: "Fine, how about this: Are you a magician? Because whenever I look at you, everyone else disappears!"

Khwaaish: "Nice attempt, but magicians are so last season. Stick to making magic in the kitchen, Chef Magician!"

Dushyant: "Ouch! I guess my humor needs a seasoning boost. Any suggestions, Comedy Critic?"

Khwaaish: "Just sprinkle a bit more wit and less vegetable jokes. Deal?"

Dushyant: "Deal! Let the comedy cooking begin! "So, Comedy Critic, what's your favorite kind of joke? I need to tailor my humor to your tastes."

Khwaaish: "I'm more into wit than puns, Chef Jokester. Surprise me with something clever!"

Dushyant: "Alright, here goes: Why did the tomato turn red?"

Khwaaish: "I don't know, why?"

Dushyant: "Because it saw the salad dressing!"

Khwaaish: "Well, that was unexpected. Points for creativity, Chef Tomato!"

Dushyant: "I'm glad I could 'ketchup' with your expectations. Any joke requests from the Tale Teller?"

Khwaaish: "Surprise me with a storytelling joke, Chef. Impress me with your literary wit."

Dushyant: "Why did the book go to therapy?"

Khwaaish: "I'm curious, why?"

Dushyant: "It had too many unresolved issues!"

Khwaaish: "Okay, Chef Jokester, you're on a roll! Keep the laughs coming."

Dushyant: "Glad you're enjoying the literary humor, Tale Teller. But I have to warn you, my cuteness quota is running low. Any requests?"

Khwaaish: "Hmm, surprise me with the cutest thing you can think of."

Dushyant: "Alright, brace yourself for the cuteness overload... If you were a cat, you'd purr-fectly steal my heart!"

Khwaaish: "Aww, that's adorable, Chef Romeo! You've successfully replenished the cuteness quota."

Dushyant: "Phew, crisis averted! Now, how about we continue our delightful banter over some good food and even better stories?"

Khwaaish: "Sounds like a plan, Chef Jokester. Let the culinary and comedic adventures continue!"

Dushyant: "Soon! Tale Teller!

She was really impressed by his abilities to express himself beautifully. Even though she was a poet herself and naturally inclined to be more expressive, she acknowledged that he nailed it with his words. His skills in communication and articulation left a lasting impression on her, showcasing his ability to convey thoughts and feelings in a captivating way. This admiration for his expressive talents became a noteworthy point in their interactions, adding a positive and appreciative aspect to their budding connection.

After a week, Dushyant messaged, "Hey Tale Teller, this time it's my turn to plan something special. Brace yourself for a surprise as I organize our next date. Get ready for some excitement!" In a playful and intriguing way, he hinted at taking charge of the plans for their upcoming meeting, injecting a sense of anticipation and excitement into their budding connection

She replied "Chef Jokester taking charge? I'm all in! Can't wait for the surprise. Bring it on!"

He rented a café for a day in Delhi for the next day.

Date #2 was on the horizon, and Dushyant, the Funny Chef, wanted to make it extra special. He messaged Khwaaish with excitement and a touch of humor.

Dushyant: "Hey Tale Teller! Get ready for Date #2 - Fun Explosion. Let's meet at 'Giggle Grill' this Saturday at 6 PM. Dress code: Smiles a must!

Khwaaish, laughing at the quirky invite, replied, "Giggle Grill it is! What's the surprise this time, Chef Jokester? Can't wait!

At 'Giggle Grill,' a place filled with laughter and good food, Dushyant, wearing a funny apron, greeted Khwaaish with a goofy bow.

Dushyant: "Welcome to the land of laughter! Today, we feast on jokes and delicious bites. Starting with 'Paneer Puns' and 'Chatpata Chaat.' Let the laughter begin!"

Khwaaish, enjoying the playful menu, said, "Chef Jokester, you really know how to cook up a good time! Let's dig into this comedy feast."

While relishing their meal- Dushyant- "And now, our surprise act! Brace yourself, Tale Teller".

He handed her a 'Mystery Masala Box' with small notes inside containing jokes and sweet compliments written by him.

Here are some notes

"If beauty were time, you'd be an eternity. Lucky for me, I've got all the time in the world to admire you."

"If beauty were a crime, you'd be serving a life sentence. Luckily for you, stealing hearts is not against the law."

"Are you a WIFI signal? Because I'm feeling a strong connection. Either that or I need to switch to decaf."

Dushyant: "A mix of laughter and a sprinkle of compliments - my secret recipe for keeping the smiles flowing."

Khwaaish, bursting into laughter, said, "Chef Jokester, you've topped yourself! This is hilarious and adorable. Thanks for such a unique date!"

The night ended with lots of laughter and a promise for more amusing adventures in the romantic comedy journey of Dushyant and Khwaaish.

While next day she texted Dushyant "OMG, the second date was like a Bollywood movie, full of surprises and laughter! Dushyant, the 'Prince Chef,' is not just a fantastic cook; you're a magician with surprises. From the Mystery Masala Box to the hilarious notes inside, I couldn't stop laughing. Your sweet compliments were like the cherry on top. Feeling grateful for this charming and entertaining date. Can't wait for the next chapter in our story!

Dushyant reply- "Haha, glad you enjoyed our little Bollywood-style adventure! You're the real magic in this story, turning every moment into a blockbuster. Your laughter is my favorite soundtrack. Ready for more surprises and laughter in our upcoming episodes? Buckle up, because this journey is just getting started."

As the days passed, the bond between Dushyant and Khwaaish deepened. Dushyant shared details about his college life with Khwaaish, and also talked about Mannat, who is his best friend. Khwaaish, in turn, shared her own experiences, discussing how she developed an interest in poetry and storytelling, and narrating stories about her school and college life. They spent hours talking, sharing everything with each other, whether it was about Khwaaish's upcoming events or Dushyant's continuous experimentation with new recipes. This constant exchange of stories and experiences strengthened their bond even more.

One day, Dushyant poured his heart out to Khwaaish, sharing the intricacies of his past, including the strained relationship with his parents. She, responding with empathy and love, reassured him: "In vulnerability, I find strength, Dushyant. Your past doesn't define you; it's the person you've become that I **love**. Your struggles are now our shared journey, and I'm here to walk every step with you. You've breathed new life into my world, and I believe in us. Together, we'll write the script of our lives with love and resilience. You're not alone anymore; I'm right here, your Khwaaish, ready to face any storm by your side."

Dushyant, who had a keen eye for details, couldn't help but notice the word "love" in Khwaaish's admission. Fueled by curiosity, he gently probed, asking, "So, Khwaaish, are you saying you love me?" In response, she candidly and vulnerably confirmed her feelings. However, Dushyant, staying true to his romantic nature, decided not to express those weighty words over texts or calls. Instead, he shared a heartfelt sentiment, acknowledging that the profound declaration of love should be reserved for a truly special occasion—one that both of them would cherish deeply for a lifetime.

Switching to a more relaxed tone, Dushyant swiftly shifted the conversation's focus. He playfully introduced the topic of Mannat's upcoming engagement, jokingly suggesting that Mannat might be disappointed if she didn't make an appearance. Transitioning smoothly, he casually inquired if she had plans for the coming Sunday, expressing that it would be wonderful if she could accompany him to the event. Dushyant highlighted that attending the engagement would not only provide an opportunity for Khwaaish to meet Mannat personally but also allow her to be part of the celebratory occasion.

Feeling a bit down, Khwaaish shared that she already had a commitment for that day – a live performance on stage. Dushyant couldn't help but feel a twinge of disappointment, realizing that Mannat might be upset, maybe even angry, if Khwaaish couldn't make it to the engagement ceremony. In an effort to resolve the situation, she suggested getting Mannat's contact so she could personally explain and apologize for her absence. She persuaded him to agree to this, even if it meant doing so somewhat reluctantly. This turn of events added a layer of concern and a hint of dilemma to the unfolding situation.

On Mannat's engagement day, Dushyant, with a sense of apology, told Mannat that he had made an effort to bring Khwaaish but she had prior commitments. Mannat, understanding and forgiving, smiled and reassured him that it was okay. In a playful manner, she jokingly imposed a lighthearted punishment on him – he had to dance alone in the spotlight as he couldn't fulfill a certain wish. Dushyant, attempting to playfully avoid the situation, found himself caught in Mannat's emotional tactics. Eventually, he agreed to dance, showing a mix of reluctance and amusement.

In the midst of the spotlight, enveloped by darkness, Dushyant was on the verge of beginning his dance when he felt a tap on his shoulder. In a state of shock and utter surprise, he turned around to discover Khwaaish standing there, dressed in a saree. Overwhelmed with emotion, he could hardly believe his eyes. Khwaaish, with a warm smile, asked him, "Shall we dance?" and Dushyant, filled with pure joy, responded, "Absolutely, my Princess."

With their hands on each other's waists, eyes gleaming, and radiant smiles, they gracefully danced together. Amidst the dance, Khwaaish let in on a secret – she and Mannat had planned the entire scenario as a playful prank. She playfully asked, "So, how did you find the surprise, my Prince Chef?"

In that moment, a surge of joy and relief swept over Dushyant. In the depths of his heart, he understood that Khwaaish was there not just for the happy times but also during the challenging moments. A subtle touch of tears formed in his eyes, moved by the profound emotions and the happiness of having someone incredibly special standing beside him. It was a realization that went beyond the dance floor, highlighting the strength and significance of the bond they shared.

Dushyant decided to make Mannat's engagement ceremony the perfect moment to propose to Khwaaish. He meticulously planned a surprise that would forever be etched in their memories. As the engagement ceremony unfolded, Dushyant approached the stage with a glint in his eye and a heart full of love. The venue was already adorned with fairy lights, creating a dreamy atmosphere. He had arranged for a small band to play soft romantic music in the background.

As he took the mic, the crowd hushed in anticipation. With a warm smile, Dushyant began to express his feelings for her. He spoke about their journey, the laughter they shared, the dreams they built together, and the unconditional support she offered.

The atmosphere was charged with love and romance. Dushyant then turned to Khwaaish, who was standing near the stage, her eyes filled with curiosity. He walked towards her, holding a bouquet of her favorite flowers. In front of everyone, Dushyant dropped down on one knee. The crowd gasped, and she covered her mouth in surprise. With heartfelt words, he asked, "Khwaaish, will you make my life as beautiful as your stories?

In the moonlit glow, where dreams unfold,

A tale of love, a story to be told.

With stars as witnesses, shining bright,

I stand before you, my heart alight.

Khwaaish, my muse, my guiding star,

In your presence, love travels far.

With every heartbeat, a whispered plea,

Will you share forever, just you and me?

Through laughter and tears, in every rhyme,

With you, forever, till the end of time.

Let's dance through life, hand in hand,

Khwaaish, will you be my forever land?

(The poem is romantic expression set in a in the moonlight, the he expresses his love for Khwaaish. He describes she as his inspiration and guiding star. He wants to be together forever, sharing both joyful and challenging moments. The idea is to dance through life hand in hand, asking if she will be their lifelong partner. It's a sweet and sincere expression of love and commitment)

Time seemed to stand still as the crowd eagerly awaited her response. Khwaaish, overwhelmed with emotions, nodded with tears of joy streaming down her face and said this.

In the dance of stars, our fates entwined,

Yes, my love, in your arms, forever bind.

The engagement ceremony transformed into a celebration of love, with Mannat's joyous engagement blending seamlessly with Dushyant and Khwaaish's beautiful new chapter.

After the engagement, Dushyant walked Khwaaish to her doorstep, feeling a surge of courage as he prepared to broach a significant question. With a deep breath, he asked, "Would you be open to meeting my parents?" To his surprise, she agreed, but with a playful twist – she insisted that he first meet her own parents. Despite the initial nerves, Dushyant accepted the challenge, and as he entered Khwaaish's home, a mix of anticipation and butterflies in his stomach overwhelmed him. However, any trepidation quickly dissolved as her parents warmly welcomed him, radiating friendliness and understanding. Their openness and kindness conveyed a deep trust in their daughter's choice, affirming to Dushyant that he was indeed the right match for Khwaaish.

Yet, amid the warm reception, a subtle yearning grew within Dushyant. He couldn't help but wish for a similar level of support and acceptance from his own parents. This encounter marked a pivotal moment in their relationship, bringing to the forefront the intricate dynamics of familial expectations and hopes.

As for the meeting with Khwaaish's parents, they, like any concerned parents, wanted to ensure the best for their daughter. They asked Dushyant about his background, aspirations, and his plans for the future. The questions were gentle but probing, reflecting the genuine concern any parent would have when their child is about to embark on a lifelong journey.

Dushyant, recognizing the significance of the moment, answered with honesty and sincerity. He shared his values, dreams, and his deep affection for Khwaaish. Khwaaish's parents, perceptive and caring, sensed his genuine intentions and the love he held for their daughter.

After the questioning, as the conversation unfolded, they gradually eased into laughter and shared anecdotes. In the end, Khwaaish's parents, convinced of Dushyant's sincerity and the love they witnessed between the couple, wholeheartedly agreed to the union. This pivotal interaction not only solidified Dushyant and Khwaaish's bond but also showcased the power of open communication and mutual understanding in navigating the delicate terrain of familial approval.

After gaining approval from Khwaaish's side, Dushyant decided to introduce her to his parents and express his desire to spend his life with her. He approached his parents and informed them about his feelings, mentioning that he wanted to marry someone he loves. His parents, initially leaning towards an arranged marriage, insisted that love marriages often lead to conflicts and unhappiness. Dushyant, determined, pointed out that even their arranged marriage didn't prevent them from fighting and being unhappy. After much persuasion, they reluctantly gave him permission to bring her home.

On same evening, When Khwaaish met Dushyant's parents, they expressed concerns about their family tradition of arranged marriages and maintaining caste norms. She, with maturity, calmly conveyed that in marriage, caste should not be the determining factor, emphasizing that such distinctions were created by people and should not dictate personal choices. She promised them that her presence would not bring any disharmony to the family, pledging to be a daughter rather than just a daughter-in-law. Her words resonated with the family, breaking the stereotype of inter-caste marriages, and they began to see her as a valuable addition to their lives.

Dushyant's father warmly welcomed her into the family, appreciating not just her outer beauty but also acknowledging her good character. Overwhelmed by the positive response, he couldn't believe the sudden change in his parents' demeanor. Intrigued, he jokingly asked her in private if she knew any magic because he had never seen his parents so happy before.

The love between Dushyant and Khwaaish blossomed, filling the air around them with an unparalleled joy. Their weekends were filled with beautiful moments spent on dates, as they both continued to strive towards their individual dreams. Each day brought them closer, and together they discovered the true essence of happiness.

One day suddenly, excitement filled the air as both decided to create a "**Wishlist**", outlining their dreams and aspirations to fulfill over time. With a spark of creativity, they sat down to brainstorm and jot down the desires that would shape their shared future. The Wishlist became a canvas for their dreams, a roadmap for the adventures they envisioned together. Little did they know, this simple act would weave a tapestry of unforgettable moments in the chapters of their lives.

With the belief in the lucky number 11, both excitedly listed their 11 wishes on boards. Each wish got its own special place, forming a visual representation of their dreams. Whenever a wish came true, they joyfully marked it with a tick and noted the date. These boards became a charming record of their shared journey, proudly displayed in their home – a testament to the magic of realizing dreams together.

Here is the list of Wishes they inked.

Wish #1- A gift to each other that is both Expensive and cheaper at the same time.

Wish #2- Five Weekend Dates without Phones

Wish #3- Wish to have a First child as a girl

Wish #4- Switching each other houses and make Dinner for a Family

Wish #5- Taking the Girl's Surname after Marriage

Wish #6- Propose in a Unique way for Marriage

Wish #7- Creating Post-Wedding Video

Wish #8- Own a Dream House

Wish #9- Having a Cat and Dog as Pets.

Wish #10- Name A Star Together

Wish #11- Write a Book on their life

As Dushyant pondered over the Wishlist, he discovered that wish #1 appeared to be a puzzle, a mystery embodying the contradiction of being both costly and affordable at the same time. The enigma fascinated him, leaving him curious about the nature of this distinctive gift. The intrigue grew as he contemplated what this one-of-a-kind item might turn out to be.

The wish #3 on the list brought about a unique set of feelings for Dushyant. The idea of their first child being a girl brought a mix of excitement and worry. He pondered the unpredictability of it all—after all, can anyone accurately predict whether the baby will be a boy or a girl before they are born? This uncertainty left him in a state of dilemma, torn between the thrill of anticipation and the anxiety of not knowing what the future holds.

In the midst of Dushyant's dilemma for same, Khwaaish responded with unwavering confidence, reassuring him that where there's a will, there's a way. Her words echoed encouragement, fostering hope in their ability to overcome challenges and turn their wishes into reality.

The next day, Mannat surprised Dushyant with the news of her upcoming wedding, and he could hardly believe that his partner in crime was finally getting married. Amidst the excitement, Mannat, true to her thrifty nature, revealed that "they couldn't afford to pay to any outsider chef, we are hiring you for chef services for free." Taking it in stride, Dushyant, always ready with a joke, burst into laughter, declaring, "Consider me your free chef! Who would've thought my cooking skills would become a form of friendship currency? I'm on board for this wedding adventure, no paycheck needed. Let's add some spice to your big day, Noddy!" Their playful banter set the stage for the comedic chaos that awaited Dushyant in his new role as the honorary wedding chef.

Dushyant shared the news of Mannat's upcoming wedding with Khwaaish, and she extended her heartfelt congratulations. Excited about the celebration, she assured that she would make it to the event, ready to join the festivities and revel in the joyous occasion.

Dushyant, overjoyed by the news of Mannat's upcoming wedding, seized the moment to ask Khwaaish a question close to his heart. With enthusiasm, he inquired, "Are you ready for our first day without phones, Tale Teller?

She agreed- **Date #1 without phones**

On their first date, Dushyant and Khwaaish decided to ditch their phones and dive into the lively heart of the city, setting the stage for a day filled with unexpected surprises and heartwarming moments.

As they strolled through the bustling streets, they stumbled upon a quaint bookstore, a haven for literary enthusiasts. Surrounded by the aroma of old books, they lost themselves in the magic of classic novels, exchanging laughter and sharing their favorite tales. It was as if the characters whispered secrets to them, and they crafted their own love story amidst the shelves, making the bookstore an unintentional cupid in their narrative.

Their impromptu adventure then led them to the vibrant art district, where murals and sculptures transformed the surroundings into a kaleidoscope of colors. A street musician serenaded them with a soulful melody, and in a whimsical turn of events, Dushyant showcased his guitar skills, turning the street into a lively stage for their own impromptu concert. Laughter echoed through the streets, and the artist in them embraced the joyous chaos of the moment.

The day gracefully transitioned into the evening, guiding them
to a charming café tucked away in a quiet corner. Illuminated by
fairy lights, the café provided the perfect ambiance for heartfelt
conversations over cups of rich, aromatic coffee. Amidst the
cozy setting, Dushyant seized the moment to unveil a poem he
had crafted just for Khwaaish, a poetic masterpiece that spilled
the emotions bubbling in his heart since their initial meeting.

Having found you, I feel as if I'm lost,

To express my feelings, at what cost?

Having found you, it's like losing my way,

What words can I say to convey?

In any language, there are no words,

To describe the essence where you're stirred.

If I were to say you're beautiful, it's true,

But in the cosmos, there's no comparison to you.

If I say you're the most exquisite,

No place in the universe can compete.

To praise you, truth be told,

There's nothing, no words to unfold.

Your presence is like a melody,

Immersed in the depths of serenity.

Your face reflects a hidden grace,

Tresses framing it, a captivating embrace.

Like waves in the ocean of charm,

Your demeanor, a soothing balm.

A cascade of locks, dense and deep,

Showering down, secrets to keep.

A radiant halo, like a moonlit night,

Enveloping you in its gentle light.

A dance of beauty in every feature,

A celestial phenomenon, a captivating creature.

If I were to paint you with words,

The canvas would be the vast sky, for sure.

With strokes of admiration and love,

A masterpiece, inspired from above.

So, let it be said in poetic decree,

In this universe, there's none like thee.

To capture your essence, try as I might,

Having found you, it's like losing in the light.

(In this heartfelt poem, he grapples with the challenge of adequately expressing the beauty and significance of her beloved. The verses convey a sense of awe and admiration, highlighting the difficulty he faces in finding words that truly capture the depth of emotions. The comparisons to celestial elements, such as the moon and the vast sky, add a poetic and romantic touch, underlining the idea that she being described is beyond ordinary description. Despite his attempts to convey his feelings, there's a recognition that some aspects of the beloved defy conventional language, making the task of expressing his uniqueness a poetic and artistic endeavor. The verses beautifully paint a picture of the loved one's charm, emphasizing the inadequacy of mere words to encapsulate the profound emotions evoked by their presence.)

As the night descended, they found themselves at a rooftop restaurant, the city's skyline serving as a breathtaking backdrop to their budding romance. Each shared glance and gentle touch added a new layer to the connection blossoming between them. The absence of phones proved to be a blessing, allowing them to be fully present, savoring each moment, and creating a treasure trove of memories that would forever mark the enchanting beginning of their love story.

In this romantic and funny escapade, the couple not only discovered the hidden gems of the city but also unearthed the magic of their connection, turning an ordinary date into an extraordinary adventure filled with laughter, music, and the sweet promise of love.

After such a magical date, Khwaaish feels a warm flutter in her heart, as if it's wrapped in a cozy blanket of joy and affection, relishing the enchanting moments and eagerly looking forward to the next chapter of their blossoming romance.

A few days later, Dushyant and Khwaaish left for Mannat's wedding. On the day of his arrival, they embraced each other, sharing heartfelt conversations. In a playful moment, Mannat, in a comic tone, suggested to get to work and make some food since Chef Dushyant was there. Playfully, he teased her by calling her "lady Hitler" and went on to prepare a delicious meal for the entire family.

Filled with joy and gratitude, Mannat expressed how she takes pride in not having many material possessions but treasures the friendship she shares with Dushyant, who has been a constant support through thick and thin. In a moment of generosity, she offered him the opportunity to make a wish, and without hesitation, he eagerly wished to give a name to her first child. Touched and teary-eyed, Mannat smiled, promising to be there for him whenever he needed support. Trying to keep the atmosphere light, Dushyant advised her not to get too emotional, and she assured him that his wish was granted. However, she playfully added a condition that the name he chooses should be good, or else she jokingly threatened, "I'll kill you." Observing the strong bond and trust between both of them, Khwaaish's heart melted, witnessing the depth of their relationship.

In Mannat's wedding, Dushyant added vibrant colors to the celebration by lighting up the gathering with dance, strumming his guitar on Friend's Sitcom Theme song, and reciting heartfelt poetry, all specially dedicated to Mannat.

In a land of laughter, where jokes take flight,

Mannat and Dushyant, a duo so bright.

With humor as their guide and puns galore,

Our friendship's a comedy, forevermore.

In jest and jesters, our bond is sealed,

Mannat's wit, Dushyant's jokes revealed.

A dynamic duo, a comic brigade,

In the comedy of life, our jokes never fade.

Through highs and lows, with laughter they cope,

Their friendship's a sitcom, a laughter-filled trope.

Mannat and Dushyant, the jesters supreme,

In the realm of comedy, they reign and beam.

(This poem celebrates the enduring friendship between Mannat and Dushyant, portraying them as a dynamic duo with a shared love for humor. The land of laughter symbolizes their joyful camaraderie, where jokes become the wings that carry them through life. The humor in their friendship is likened to a comedy, a perpetual sitcom, highlighting the comedic elements that define their bond. Through highs and lows, their laughter-filled camaraderie stands resilient, making Mannat and Dushyant the jesters supreme in the comedy of life.)

Surrounded by a joyful and rhythmic atmosphere, the wedding celebrations became even more memorable. Amidst the festivities, Dushyant proudly brings Khwaaish along, introducing her to everyone as his "**Lifeline.**" Blushing, she teases him, claiming he's now giving her a tough competition in the poetry department. Dushyant laughs and playfully grabs his ear, insisting that he can never surpass her. Turning to the gathered audience, he asks, "So, my dear audience, if you want to hear her recite a poem, give me a cheer!" The crowd enthusiastically cheers, and Khwaaish, in response to their excitement, recites a heartfelt poem, adding a touch of her poetic charm to the wedding celebration.

In the realm of bonds, where friendships bloom,

Mannat and Dushyant, a duo that lights up the room.

A tale spun with laughter, a melody so sweet,

In the book of camaraderie, their story finds its seat.

Dushyant, the chef, with flavors so divine,

Mannat, his partner, in the rhythm of rhyme.

Together they dance, in joy and in jest,

A friendship that's enduring, a bond truly blessed.

In the canvas of moments, where memories unfold,

Mannat and Dushyant, their story is told.

With every shared laughter, and every heartfelt cheer,

Khwaaish weaves poetry, celebrating friendships dear.

So, here's to the trio, a friendship so bright,

In the chapters of life, they continue to write.

With Mannat, Dushyant, and Khwaaish's sweet rhyme,

Their story echoes through the corridors of time.

(This poem celebrates the enduring friendship of Mannat, Dushyant, and Khwaaish, portraying them as a radiant trio that illuminates the realm of bonds. The verses depict their camaraderie, with Mannat and Dushyant as a dynamic duo bringing light and laughter. Dushyant, the chef, adds a divine flavor, and Mannat contributes to the rhythm of shared experiences. The poem highlights their enduring and blessed friendship, with Khwaaish, the poet, weaving their story into verses. The trio's bright friendship continues to unfold in the chapters of life, echoing through the corridors of time as a testament to enduring connections.)

Speaking to the gathered audience with a lively whistle, Dushyant joyfully declared, "I've been proclaiming it for all to hear — she's the master, and I'm nothing more than her dedicated apprentice."

They all embraced in a group hug, capturing a candid moment filled with warmth and friendship.

Dushyant playfully inquired, "Shall we carry on with our tradition of a second date without phones? The opportunity is here, and so is the ritual!"

Khwaaish replied with a smile, "Absolutely! Let's continue our tradition of a second date without phones. Looking forward to another memorable day with you."

Date #2 Without Phone

In the lively atmosphere of Mannat's wedding, where joyous celebrations echoed and vibrant colors adorned every corner, Dushyant and Khwaaish seized a moment to escape the bustling crowd. Amidst the rhythmic beats of music and the laughter of friends and family, they found a quiet corner, creating an impromptu haven for a unique and spontaneous date.

Dushyant, the culinary maestro, decided to add a sweet twist to the occasion. With a mischievous sparkle in his eyes, he presented Khwaaish with a plate of handcrafted sweets, each a masterpiece of flavors that titillated the taste buds. As they savored the delightful treats, the air around them seemed to carry the sweetness of the moment.

Feeling the infectious energy of the wedding, they decided to join the dance floor, where the DJ spun a mix of peppy tracks and soulful melodies. In the midst of swirling colors and flashing lights, Dushyant and Khwaaish danced like no one was watching. The DJ, sensing the connection between them, even played their favorite song, turning the dance into a delightful, intimate affair.

As they swayed in the dance, Dushyant whispered these sweet words softly into Khwaaish's ear.

"Your wonderful 'yes' has opened up a new and beautiful chapter in the story of our love, making every moment we share feel like something out of a magical fairy tale, where dreams come true. When you agreed and said 'yes,' it felt like a brand-new love song started playing in my heart, and I can't wait to create the sweetest melodies with you, turning each day into a harmonious symphony of our affection. The sparkle in your eyes after saying 'yes' revealed a love that shines even brighter than the stars in the night sky, filling my heart with excitement for the amazing journey we're about to embark on together. With your 'yes,' you've given me the incredible gift of being your forever, and I'm eagerly looking forward to starting a journey where we build beautiful memories together, creating a tapestry of moments that will last a lifetime."

As they swayed to the music, the laughter and cheers of the wedding guests merged with their own joyful voices. Amidst the celebration, Dushyant and Khwaaish discovered a deeper connection, the bond of their hearts syncing with the beats of the music. The wedding ambiance added a touch of magic to their date, making it a momentous chapter in their blossoming love story. In the midst of wedding revelry, they carved out a space for their own romance, creating memories that would linger in their hearts for a lifetime. Date #2 without phones finally ended.

As the final notes of celebration faded away, and the wedding concluded with heartfelt goodbyes, the newlyweds, Mannat and her partner, were left with the promise of a beautiful journey ahead. However, one surprise awaited them – a thoughtful and extravagant wedding gift from both of them.

The couple, who shared a bond that transcended friendship, decided to sponsor Mannat's honeymoon as a gesture of love and blessings. Their generous gift included a curated travel package to a breathtaking destination, ensuring that the newlyweds embarked on a romantic and memorable journey to kickstart their married life.

Mannat, overwhelmed with gratitude, couldn't believe the extent of their generosity. She hugged Khwaaish and Dushyant tightly, expressing her heartfelt appreciation for such a thoughtful and extravagant gift. The gesture not only showcased the depth of their friendship but also added a touch of magic to Mannat's new chapter of life.

With bags packed and hearts full of excitement, Mannat and her partner set off on their dream honeymoon, cherishing the warmth and affection of their dear friends who had made their special day even more extraordinary. The bond between Mannat, Khwaaish, and Dushyant continued to grow, weaving a tapestry of friendship, love, and shared adventures that would last a lifetime.

As the newlyweds settled into their post-wedding bliss, Mannat felt an overwhelming sense of gratitude. Unable to contain her joy, she decided to make a heartfelt call to them expressing her appreciation for the extraordinary gift they had bestowed upon her and her partner.

Mannat, with a tone filled with warmth and happiness, shared how the honeymoon experience was turning out to be a dream come true. The scenic beauty, the romantic ambiance, and the precious moments created an enchanting backdrop for their new journey together. She couldn't thank both of them enough for making this once-in-a-lifetime experience possible.

Khwaaish and Dushyant, on the other end of the call, felt immense joy hearing Mannat's excitement. Their intention was to add a sprinkle of magic to the beginning of Mannat's married life, and it seemed like their mission was accomplished. Her words of gratitude echoed the strength of their friendship and the bonds that tied them together.

As the conversation unfolded, she also shared snippets of her honeymoon adventures, the laughter, and the quiet romantic moments that would become cherished memories. The call became a virtual bridge connecting the trio, even in the midst of physical distances.

Little did they know that this thoughtful gift and the subsequent call were just the beginning of a series of shared adventures and celebrations that awaited them in the journey of friendship and love.

After hearing this-

Khwaaish gazed at Dushyant, her eyes reflecting a myriad of emotions. In that moment, she realized what an incredible gem she had found in her life. As she observed him, perhaps lost in own thoughts or engaged in the simple joys of life, she couldn't help but feel grateful for the bond they shared. It was more than a love; it was a tapestry woven with threads of understanding, trust, and an unspoken connection that transcended words.

The chef who added flavors to her life, the storyteller who painted vivid tales with words, and the person whose presence brought warmth to her heart — he was, indeed, a gem that sparkled brightly in the mosaic of her existence.

The realization filled Khwaaish's heart with a gentle warmth, a reassurance that in Dushyant, she had a companion who stood not only as a friend but as a precious jewel illuminating the path of their journey together.

The next morning, she pleasantly surprised Dushyant by visiting his house. With a mysterious gleam in her eyes, she hinted at having a special surprise for him. Intrigued, Dushyant welcomed her with a warm smile, curious about the nature of the surprise.

As they stood in his living room, she instructed him to close his eyes and turn to face the opposite direction. She began counting to three, and as he turned, he found himself standing in front of a mirror. A puzzled expression adorned his face as he wondered what kind of surprise involved a mirror.

With a mischievous yet affectionate tone, she explained, "Remember our first wish – a gift to each other that is both expensive and cheaper at the same time?" She pointed towards the mirror and continued, "This reflection in this mirror, my dear, is your gift. So, you can see a reflection of the most expensive and valuable person in my life in this cheap mirror— you."

Dushyant, touched by the simplicity and depth of the surprise, looked at himself in the mirror with newfound appreciation. A soft smile formed on Dushyant's face as he continued to gaze into the mirror. He turned to her, his eyes reflecting appreciation and affection. Without uttering a word, he pulled her into a warm embrace, expressing his gratitude for the beautiful and meaningful gift she had given him. In that moment, their connection deepened, and the mirror became a symbol of the precious bond they shared.

Following that, she suggested, "How about our third date without the interference of phones?"

Dushyant smiled warmly and responded, "Absolutely, my Tale Teller. You lead the way."

"Underneath the vast canvas of the starlit sky, she transformed the car into a haven of love. Soft, ambient music played in the background, creating a melody that echoed through the quiet night. The car was adorned with fairy lights, casting a warm glow on their faces.

As they settled into the cozy space, she handed him a personalized playlist. Each song had a special meaning, carefully chosen to reflect the cadence of their journey together. The rhythmic hum of the engine blended seamlessly with the soulful tunes, setting the stage for a night to remember.

Khwaaish, a true poet at heart, had written a heartfelt letter expressing her emotions. Tied with a ribbon, the letter awaited Dushyant on the dashboard. The car became a vessel for their deepest thoughts, carrying them through a journey of shared dreams and aspirations. The letter contained this below poetry.

In dreams of youth, I dared to scheme,

A life with you, a cherished dream.

Now here we stand, reality spun,

Childhood visions brought to the sun.

Your smile, a radiant beam of light,

A starlit laughter, a celestial delight.

Each day, a canvas of colors anew,

Simple moments painted, extraordinary and true.

Together we venture, an adventure untold,

Life's mysteries unravel, a tale to be scrolled.

Falling in love, a perpetual refrain,

Each dawn brings a love born again.

(The above poem portrays- Being with you is like stepping into a dream that I never thought would come true, especially considering the dreams I used to have when I was a kid. But here we are, and I'm so grateful for you turning those childhood dreams into real moments. Your smile is like sunshine to me, and when you laugh, it's as if the stars in the sky are twinkling. Every day with you is a new adventure, turning ordinary moments into extraordinary ones. It's like we're on this exciting journey together, and I can't wait to see where life takes us. Falling in love with you happens all over again each day, and it's the most incredible feeling. Your love is like a special kind of magic, filled with passion and kindness, making my life better in ways I never imagined. I just want you to know how thankful I am for everything.)

The night air whispered sweet secrets as they drove along scenic routes, the moonlight casting a silvery glow on their faces. She had also packed a picnic basket filled with their favorite snacks and a thermos of hot coffee, turning the car into a movable feast of love.

As they parked at a secluded spot, she encouraged him to stargaze through the sunroof. She pointed out constellations, weaving tales in the celestial tapestry above. The car became a portal to a universe where their love story unfolded against the backdrop of twinkling stars.

The date was a symphony of romantic gestures, combining music, poetry, and the beauty of the night sky. Khwaaish's creativity knew no bounds, making this car date an enchanting chapter in the book of their shared experiences."

Dushyant was utterly enchanted by her thoughtful arrangements for their car date. The heartfelt letter touched Dushyant deeply. He read it with a mixture of joy and gratitude, realizing the depth of Khwaaish's feelings for him. Grateful for her creativity and the effort she had invested, Dushyant responded with genuine appreciation. He expressed how the date had touched his heart, making him feel incredibly special. In that moment, he knew that their journey was filled with countless more chapters of love and enchantment. Date #3 there ended.

After pondering for a couple of days on what precious yet affordable gift to give Khwaaish, Dushyant had an epiphany. He thought about it from her perspective and tried to understand what she might appreciate as a thoughtful and budget-friendly gesture.

Dushyant, with a glint of excitement in his eyes, approached Khwaaish's house, holding his carefully crafted surprise. As he stood before her, he hinted at the anticipation of the unique gift he had in store for her.

Khwaaish, intrigued and curious, asked about the surprise. He, with a mischievous smile, replied, "It's something unique, valuable, and yet, quite affordable." She pressed for more details, eager to unravel the mystery.

"Close your eyes," he said, gently taking her hand in his. "Now, give me your hand, and feel this," he instructed, placing her hand on his chest. "Can you sense something?" he asked.

With closed eyes, Khwaaish felt the rhythmic thumping beneath her hand. "Your heartbeat," she remarked, a touch of realization in her voice.

Dushyant beamed, "Exactly. I searched high and low for a valuable gift, not realizing that I already possess the most precious thing – my heart. Now, it belongs to you. What was inexpensive within me, when gifted to you, makes me feel like the richest person on this planet. Please, cherish it."

In the realm of love, a gift so rare,

I placed my heart in your tender care.

Handle it gently, like petals so fine,

In the garden of love, forever entwined.

Safe within the haven of your embrace,

With each heartbeat, our love takes its pace.

Promises whispered in the moonlit night,

A symphony of love, pure and bright.

I pledge to be there, day after day,

In the dance of stars, our love will sway.

A promise unbroken, forever to keep,

In the vast expanse, where dreams and love seep.

So, hold my heart, delicate and true,

A treasure bestowed, solely for you.

In this romance, our spirits entwine,

A poetic love, forever divine.

(In this poem, he expresses the rarity of love, entrusting their heart to a beloved. The verses evoke the image of delicate petals in a love garden, emphasizing the tender care the heart seeks. The embrace is portrayed as a haven, where love's symphony unfolds in moonlit promises. He pledges enduring presence and promises unbroken, dancing through the vast expanse of dreams and love. The heart is offered as a precious treasure in this poetic and divine romance. The essence lies in the enduring commitment and the intertwining of spirits in a love that is forever pure and bright.)

Khwaaish was deeply moved by Dushyant's heartfelt gift, realizing that the most valuable and precious thing he could offer was his own heart. As he asked her to feel his heartbeat, she sensed the sincerity and love within his gesture, making the moment truly special for both of them.

With exchanged gifts of a mirror and a heartfelt promise, both joyfully fulfilled their first wish. The mirror reflected the beauty of their connection, while Dushyant's promise to cherish and keep heart safe marked the beginning of a journey filled with love and happiness. As they smiled through tears, they proudly ticked off the first item on their shared Wishlist.

Wish #1- A gift to each other that is both Expensive and cheaper at the same time i.e Khwaaish's Gift- Mirror and Dushyant's Gift- His own Heart- Completed

Overflowing with enthusiasm to fulfill their next wish of exchanging homes and preparing dinner for each other's families, Khwaaish and Dushyant joyfully embarked on an exciting culinary adventure. She, armed with plans to recreate the beloved dishes of Dushyant's family, and Dushyant, showcasing his culinary expertise, geared up for a delightful kitchen experience. Despite Dushyant's eagerness to offer hands-on assistance, she politely declined, expressing her desire to independently impress his family with her culinary skills. Instead, she welcomed his valuable tips and tricks, fostering an atmosphere of collaboration and anticipation in their shared cooking endeavor.

As the final day arrived, she prepared a sumptuous feast of Biryani and cheesecake for Dushyant's family. Dushyant, feeling the pressure and unable to assist, could only pray for the success of this culinary endeavor. she, determined to prove herself, cooked every dish independently, serving it to Dushyant's family with a mix of excitement and nervousness.

The moment of truth came when Dushyant's parents took the first bite. Both anxiously awaited their reaction. The room fell silent as his parents savored the flavors. To their relief and delight, his parents beamed with joy, praising the delicious feast. Both exchanged relieved glances, realizing that she had not only passed the test but also won the hearts of his family.

Later, as Dushyant took a bite himself, he was pleasantly surprised at the delectable taste. Whispers of "Bingo! You made it, Tale Teller" confirmed her culinary success, and he couldn't have been prouder of her accomplishment.

His father gives her a token of good luck, acknowledging that she has cooked her first meal, following an Indian tradition and she took his parents blessings.

Next Weekend, it was now Mr. Perfect Chef's turn to venture into Khwaaish's kitchen and showcase his culinary prowess. However, she added an exciting twist to the game. She demanded unique recipe and names that recipe that he had never encountered before, and mischievously snatched away his phone, leaving him without any external assistance. Undeterred, he embraced the challenge, determined to craft a culinary masterpiece. She wished him the best of luck, playfully saying, "All the best, Mr. Chef. We'll reconvene at the dining table to savor your creation."

He experienced a moment of shock, wondering if this was the same girl he loved, but quickly shifted his focus to the task at hand and got busy in the kitchen, preparing the meal. As the time approached to reveal Mr. Chef's creation for her family, everyone was surprised to see the perfectly cooked dish. She, in disbelief, questioned how he accomplished it. With a cheeky smile, he attributed it to "magic," but then confessed that he

was a trained chef who knew almost all recipes. He clarified that
during the task, he pretended not to recognize the dish's name.
Uncle and Aunty were invited to taste the dish and provide their
verdict. As expected, they both awarded him a perfect score of
10 out of 10. She playfully teased Dushyant with a funny face,
and he responded with a warm smile.

As they savored the delightful meal prepared by Dushyant for
her family, the atmosphere in the room became infused with
warmth and joy. The fragrant aroma of the carefully crafted
dishes filled the air, creating a sense of togetherness and
celebration.

After the last bite was relished, they retreated to a cozy corner
of the room, where the flickering candlelight cast a soft glow.
The room seemed to hold its breath as they gazed at each
other, the silence speaking volumes.

Dushyant, overcome with a surge of emotions, took her hands
in his, the touch conveying a depth of connection beyond
words. Their eyes locked, sharing a language only they could
understand. It was a moment suspended in time, where the
unspoken promise of a lifetime together lingered in the air.

Khwaaish, with a tender smile, expressed her gratitude for the
magical evening. "Thank you, my Mr. Perfect Chef, for turning
this simple meal into a memory etched in my heart. Each day
with you feels like a step closer to falling in love more deeply.
Our journey, marked by these small wishes, has a charm of its
own.

Dushyant, reciprocating the sentiment, whispered, "These
simple moments, these wishes we've ticked off together, are
the threads weaving our love story. I look forward to the day

when every wish on our list is fulfilled, and hearts overflow with the joy of shared dreams. Thank you for making every day special, my Tale Teller.

As they embraced, the room echoed with the melody of their love, a symphony composed by the heartbeats resonating in unison. The Wishlist, now more than a mere list, became a testament to the beautiful journey they were crafting, one wish at a time.

Wish #4- Switching each other houses and make Dinner for a Family- Completed.

Out of eleven, the two wishes on their Wishlist, have been successfully completed now.

Chapter 3- Shattered Dreams

One day, as life's whirlwind of activities surrounded them, Dushyant felt a moment of reflection creeping in. In this contemplative state, he turned to Mannat for advice on a matter that held immense significance for him – the purchase of a ring for Khwaaish, his cherished partner. Unlike her usual lively and energetic self, Mannat's tone seemed a bit subdued when she answered his call. Filled with concern, Dushyant gently inquired about her well-being.

Mannat, not wanting to burden him, downplayed her condition, citing a minor illness that required nothing more than some rest and medication. When Dushyant suggested calling her husband for assistance, Mannat quickly dismissed the idea, stating that he must be busy. The conversation shifted gears as Dushyant shared his plan to propose to Khwaaish for marriage and the need for a unique ring. Mannat, finding the situation adorable, offered her assistance once she felt better.

After a short conversation, they made plans to meet in two days, giving Mannat some time to recover. Dushyant, being the thoughtful friend, suggested picking her up for their meeting. However, Mannat, always independent and strong-willed, insisted that she could make her own way there. Eventually, they settled on a convenient time, deciding to meet at 7 pm in the evening.

Two days later, Dushyant and Mannat met, but this time, an unusual tension hung in the air. Dushyant, bubbling with excitement about the ring purchase, couldn't ignore the visible shift in Mannat's usual cheerful demeanor. Her vibrant spirit seemed dimmed, and he sensed that something was bothering her.

After procuring the ring, they decided to take a seat at a nearby café. The atmosphere was heavy with unspoken concerns, and Dushyant, unable to contain his worry, gently probed Mannat about her apparent distress. He could tell that her attempt to put on a brave front and pretend everything was fine was far from convincing.

In a heartfelt moment, Dushyant, genuinely concerned, approached Mannat, conveying his worry and offering reassurance that he was ready to listen. Mannat, teary-eyed, took a moment before sharing the painful challenges she had been grappling with over the last three months. With a heavy heart, she disclosed a heartbreaking truth – her husband had heartlessly ejected her from their once-shared home.

As Mannat unfolded the painful chapters of her life, she disclosed the unsettling aspects of an abusive relationship. Her husband, beyond inflicting physical violence, had betrayed their marriage vows through an extramarital affair, driving her to the edge. Confronted with emotional and physical anguish, Mannat summoned courage to break free. She bravely chose to distance herself from the toxic environment, recognizing the need to escape the clutches of an abusive relationship. She realized that he had concealed his true self behind a mask, and his real colors were revealed only after they got married.

Dushyant, deeply affected by Mannat's revelation, assured her of his unwavering support. Mannat shared that she kept this painful truth hidden to avoid burdening him. Now aware of the harsh reality, Dushyant contemplated how to be a pillar of strength for her. Mannat expressed the need for legal assistance to secure a separation and a divorce, emphasizing her desire to handle the situation independently. She rented an apartment to stay alone, resisting pressure from her parents to move in with them. Mannat acknowledged her mistake and was determined to navigate this challenging phase on her own, not wanting to burden her family.

After a heartfelt conversation, Dushyant dropped Mannat off at her apartment. Concerned for her well-being, he offered reassurance, telling her to take care and reminding her that he was just a call away. Comforted by his words, Mannat smiled and expressed her gratitude. As she made her way towards her apartment, she carried a mix of emotions, knowing she had a supportive friend ready to stand by her side during the challenging times ahead.

The very next day, burdened by the weight of Mannat's distressing revelation, Dushyant sought solace in confiding in Khwaaish. As he shared her heartbreaking story, Khwaaish's face mirrored the sorrow and empathy that engulfed her heart.

Dushyant, grappling with the desire to support Mannat in the best possible way, explained the complexities of her situation. Khwaaish, her compassionate nature shining through, immediately offered a glimmer of hope. "My father is an advocate," she shared with him. "He has expertise in legal matters. If she is willing, I can talk to my father, and he might be able to guide her through the legal process and offer the support she needs.

Gratitude and relief washed over Dushyant as he realized the significance of this offer. With Khwaaish's father potentially providing legal assistance, Mannat could find the strength and resources to navigate the challenging path towards liberation from her troubled marriage. The alliance between Dushyant, Khwaaish, and her father became a ray of hope in Mannat's stormy journey, promising the possibility of a brighter future.

As the legal processes progressed, Mannat experienced a sense of liberation from the weight of her past struggles. Now she is officially free from burden which she was carrying on her shoulder from last three months.

Brimming with gratitude, she openly conveyed her sincere thanks to Dushyant and Khwaaish, recognizing the immense support they provided. "I feel incredibly lucky to have friends like you," she conveyed, a profound sense of indebtedness evident in her words. She expressed a wish for a world where more people displayed the same level of compassion, believing it could make the world a better place.

In a poignant moment, Mannat embraced both of them recognizing the profound impact they had on her journey to freedom. "I owe you both more than words can convey," she whispered, her eyes reflecting newfound hope and gratitude.

Dushyant, known for his ability to lighten the mood, couldn't resist adding a touch of humor to the moment. He added I have a surprise for you Mannat. She said jokingly "Is this another surprise groom you've brought for me?" Laughter echoed in response.

In the car, Dushyant presented - a fluffy bundle of joy in the form of an adorable kitten. Mannat, moved by the thoughtful gesture, couldn't contain her emotions and exclaimed, "How did you understand me so perfectly, Noddy?" Overflowing with gratitude for the joy Dushyant had brought into her life, Mannat decided to let him name the newfound feline friend. After pondering for a couple of minutes, Dushyant affectionately named the kitten "Martha," solidifying the bond between them and creating a heartwarming memory.

With a warm hug, Mannat conveyed her appreciation, "Nice name. You've given me not just a companion but a source of joy. Thank you." As Martha nestled in Mannat's arms, a symbol of newfound happiness, the duo embarked on a journey of shared laughter and brighter days ahead.

Khwaaish's eyes glistened with tears as she looked at Dushyant, her heart brimming with emotions. "You're a born giver," she whispered, her voice filled with gratitude. "I feel so blessed around you. I love you." Dushyant, with a playful smile, interrupted her heartfelt moment. "Wait, wait, hold your horses. I have a surprise for you as well—what about date #4, without phones?" he proposed.

A mix of surprise and joy danced in her eyes as she processed the unexpected offer. "Now?" she asked, seeking confirmation. Dushyant, ever the master of surprises, nodded affirmatively. "Yes, of course," he replied. Khwaaish, with a beaming smile, embraced the spontaneity of the moment. "Okay. I love your surprises, Mr. Perfect Chef," she declared, eagerly anticipating the magic that awaited them on their fourth phone-free date.

As they arrived at their destination, both stepped out of the car and left their phones behind. To Khwaaish's delight, they found themselves at a Pet Adoption and Voluntary Center. Overwhelmed with joy, she looked at Dushyant with a playful expression. "You Cutie Pie," she teased, "you know how to win my heart."

The evening unfolded at the Pet Adoption and Voluntary Center, where Dushyant and Khwaaish immersed themselves in the world of furry friends. As they entered the center, the air buzzed with excitement, and the playful antics of animals could be heard in the background.

They decided to start their date by volunteering to feed and play with the animals. Laughter filled the air as mischievous puppies and kittens darted around, bringing smiles to their faces. The couple, surrounded by adorable companions, found joy in every moment.

After spending quality time with the animals, Dushyant suggested a stroll to a nearby park where coffee awaited them. They found a cozy spot surrounded by nature, the aroma of freshly brewed coffee mingling with the sweet scent of blooming flowers. The playful atmosphere of the park mirrored the lightheartedness of their connection.

Seated on a park bench, Dushyant and Khwaaish couldn't help but notice the amusing antics of the animals around them. They shared laughs, exchanged funny names for the creatures, and basked in the simple joy of each other's company.

As the date neared its end, a surprise awaited Khwaaish. A mysterious figure approached, holding a basket adorned with a ribbon. Handing it to Khwaaish, the stranger said, "This is for you." With curiosity and excitement, she opened the basket to find a cute white puppy inside.

Dushyant, with a twinkle in his eye, revealed, "It's a gift for you, my Tale Teller." Overwhelmed with emotion, she expressed her love and gratitude for this heartwarming gesture. Dushyant, in his poetic style, suggested, "Why don't you give this adorable companion a name?"

After a moment's thought, she exclaimed, "Snow!" Dushyant couldn't hide his delight and said, "Purrrfect choice." As they embraced, surrounded by the serenity of the park and the newfound joy of their furry friend, the date became a chapter in their love story filled with laughter, surprises, and the promise of shared adventures with Snow.

Phone free Date# 4 ended.

Dushyant continued his routine of spending time with Mannat, ensuring that she didn't feel alone in her daily life. Every day, he shared snippets of his own experiences, joys, and challenges, creating a bridge that connected their lives.

In his conversations with Mannat, Dushyant often found solace in discussing the vibrant and cheerful moments he shared with Khwaaish. He would recount their adventures, the laughter they shared, and the simple joys that colored their days.

Khwaaish, being aware of Mannat's situation, suggested to Dushyant that they should make an effort to be a source of support for her. Together, they aimed to bring a sense of cheerfulness and happiness into Mannat's life. Dushyant, with his caring nature, embraced this responsibility with open arms.

Whether it was a funny incident that happened during the day or a heartwarming story, Dushyant made sure to share it with Mannat. In return, Mannat found comfort in these conversations, feeling a sense of companionship that helped alleviate the solitude she often felt.

As they navigated through life's ups and downs together, the bond between Dushyant, Khwaaish, and Mannat grew stronger. Each day became an opportunity to bring a smile to Mannat's face, reminding her that she was not alone in her journey.

Eager to make their next wish come true, Dushyant and Khwaaish set their sights on a celestial endeavor—"**Naming a star together**". A sense of anticipation and romantic excitement filled the air as they embarked on this cosmic adventure, ready to etch their love story into the vast expanse of the night sky.

In India, the process of naming a star involves engaging with specialized star-naming services that provide a unique identifier for a particular celestial body. Both began their journey by researching reputable star-naming companies that operate within the country. They wanted a service that not only provided the symbolic act of naming a star but also offered a tangible connection to the night sky.

After careful consideration, they selected a service that not only allowed them to choose a name for their star but also provided detailed information about its location in the night sky. The anticipation of having their own celestial point of light with a unique moniker, "Stardust Serenade," filled them with joy.

The process typically involves the following steps:

Research and Choose a Service: Dushyant and Khwaaish explored various star-naming services, considering factors like credibility, reviews, and the comprehensiveness of the package offered.

Selecting a Star: Once they settled on a service, they browsed through a star catalog or used online tools to locate a star that resonated with them. The coordinates and other relevant details were provided by the chosen service.

Naming the Star: With the perfect star in sight, they bestowed upon it the name that encapsulated the essence of their love – "Stardust Serenade." This name would forever be associated with that celestial body.

Customization Options: Some services offer additional customization options, such as adding a personal message or selecting a specific date for the star's registration. Dushyant and Khwaaish took advantage of these options to make their experience even more special.

Documentation: The chosen service provided documentation certifying the registration of the star, along with a star map indicating its location in the night sky. This tangible evidence of their celestial union added a beautiful touch to the entire process.

Once they completed all the necessary steps, Dushyant and Khwaaish received official documentation affirming that their chosen star, "Stardust Serenade," had now been uniquely identified in the vast cosmos. This symbolic act of naming a star transcended the earthly realm, becoming a poetic representation of their lasting love. It stood as a luminous tribute to the celestial dance of their hearts, a shimmering symbol in the cosmic tapestry of their shared journey.

Standing under the canvas of the night sky, Dushyant and Khwaaish found themselves in a moment where words were woven into the fabric of the cosmos. As they gazed at the celestial beauty, a gentle breeze carrying the essence of stardust whispered around them.

Dushyant, his eyes reflecting the brilliance of the named star, turned to Khwaaish with a tender smile. "Stardust Serenade," he murmured, the name rolling off his tongue like a poetic melody. "Just like this star in the vast expanse, our love shines brightly, leaving an indelible mark on the universe."

Khwaaish, her eyes reflecting the shimmer of the newly christened celestial companion, responded with a warmth that transcended the earthly realm. "Dushyant, with every twinkle of 'Stardust Serenade,' I feel our connection reaching beyond the heavens. This star, our star, is a testament to the infinity of our love, a love that echoes through the cosmos.

In the quietude of that celestial moment, they exchanged vows silently, promises written in the language of the stars. Their hearts, now entwined with the luminous threads of the night, spoke a language that needed no translation.

As they held each other beneath the celestial canopy, 'Stardust Serenade' became not just a name but a celestial witness to their journey—a journey illuminated by the radiance of their shared dreams and aspirations. In the silence of the night, their love echoed through the cosmos, leaving an eternal imprint on the canvas of the universe.

As both of them stepped back into the warmth of their room, a sense of fulfillment and joy lingered in the air. The celestial dance of 'Stardust Serenade' had woven a new chapter into the tapestry of their shared wishes. With a smile that mirrored the constellations, they turned to each other, and in unison, they reached for the Wishlist.

Their fingers traced the outlines of the wishes, finding solace in the simple act of checking off another wish they had nurtured together. The pen met the paper, creating a mark that transcended the boundaries of ink and parchment. The completed wish stood as a testament to their journey—a journey that embraced the magic of the ordinary and transformed it into extraordinary moments.

Dushyant, his eyes reflecting the glow of the night sky, whispered, "One more wish, my Tale Teller, etched into the cosmic tale we're writing together." Khwaaish, her gaze meeting his, replied, "Yes, one more wish fulfilled, and a universe of dreams left to explore. Our journey is a constellation of shared wishes, each one lighting up our path."

Wish #10- Name A Star Together – Completed

Next day, Dushyant excitedly shared the news with Mannat, "Guess what? We've ticked off three wishes, and the fourth one is on its way! She said your happiness means a lot but sometimes, I feel envy from you, my love birds. You both are such a perfect couple. He asked by the way, how's your quest for a companion going? Any luck in finding someone as amazing as Martha?"

Mannat, with a mischievous smile, replied, "Oh, please! I'm not actively searching. But if you can find someone as entertaining as you, I might consider it."

Dushyant laughed, "Challenge accepted! I'll put up a 'Partner in Mischief Wanted' sign. Let's see who shows up."

Mannat chuckled, "Good luck with that, Noddy. Just make sure they can survive your cooking experiments!"

Dushyant saluted dramatically, "Noted, Captain Mannat! Together, we shall embark on the quest for the perfect partners in mischief."

Laughter filled as he asked Mannat to give an idea for their next date, as he was blanked out, he couldn't think of anything. After researching for one minute, she said what about surprising Khwaaish with a Terrace Date. He said what an idea Noddy, thank you and love you, now I have to work on this idea. Bye, take care!

Next Day Dushyant texted to Khwaaish, be available tonight and come at my house along with Puppy "Snow", I had to tell you something important about my life. She was surprised what he is going to tell me now, he didn't fully unwrap himself. She was curious to know and said OKAY I'll be there.

When she reached at his house on the door- a sticky note found on which it was written. Step upwards to Terrace and left your phone at table in the room.

On the terrace, bathed in the soft glow of fairy lights, Dushyant choreographed a date that would rival the most romantic scenes from a movie. The chilly night air was enlivened by a crackling bonfire, casting a warm hue over the entire setup.

As she stepped onto the terrace with adorable puppy, Snow, wagging its tail in excitement she was greeted by the flickering flames. Dushyant, with a mischievous grin, said, "I thought our date could use a little extra warmth, so Snow is here to spread some puppy love."

The trio, with Snow playfully darting around, settled around the bonfire. Dushyant, armed with a guitar, started strumming the chords to Ed Sheeran's "Perfect." He looked at her and jokingly said, "I hope I'm more in tune than Snow's playful barks."

Laughter filled the air as Dushyant attempted to serenade her, occasionally getting interrupted by Snow's adorable antics. The Snow, seemingly inspired by the music, decided to join the performance with a series of enthusiastic yips.

As the night progressed, Dushyant revealed his culinary prowess by preparing Khwaaish's favorite meal right there on the terrace. Amidst the laughter, music, and the aromatic waft of delicious food, they enjoyed a magical evening, creating memories that would be etched in their hearts forever. Underneath the star-studded sky, surrounded by the warmth of the bonfire and the joyous energy of their furry companion, both found themselves lost in the enchantment of the moment.

In the warmth of the moment, she extended her gratitude, saying, "You're my comfort," to which he replied with a gentle smile, "And you're my constant tale teller." She reminisced about the first day they met, saying, "I was your crush, and now it seems I see you as my forever crush. Please don't change. Whether I gain weight or become fluffy, give me the same love you carry within yourself."

Dushyant, looking into her eyes, affirmed, "Indeed, I've already given you my heart, Tale Teller." He then hesitated for a moment before asking, "Can I ask you something?" Khwaaish, with an affectionate smile, replied, "Anything, my Mr. Perfect Chef."

Dushyant, with a playful twinkle in his eye, confessed, "I am having a craving to listen to your poetry. It's been a long time. Please?" In response, she leaned in, kissed him gently on the forehead, and said, "Yes, of course, my man. It's for you, always."

How did I find you, fate I couldn't believe?

Descended into life like the moon to a tranquil eve.

Softly, slowly, like the gentle sunlight's touch,

In your melody, I found solace, oh, how much!

You touched me like a breeze, a whisper in the air,

A serenade of destiny, beyond compare.

You became my peace, my unwavering passion,

Why did you not come sooner, my heart's sweet sensation?

How did I find you, fate I couldn't believe?

A journey into love, a tapestry to weave.

You are my tranquility, my fervent obsession,

In the symphony of life, you're my melodic confession.

(This heartfelt poem expresses the profound and serendipitous nature of finding love. She marvels at the seemingly fateful encounter, describing it as a descent into life akin to the moon's gentle appearance on a tranquil evening. The presence of the loved one is likened to soothing elements like sunlight and breeze, bringing solace and a sense of destiny. The poem reflects

Dushyant becomes overwhelmingly happy upon hearing her poetry, and he grabs her, swaying gently to the tunes of a song. Softly, they start a couple's dance. Whispering into her ears, he says, "Tale Teller, our fourth wish has come true – **5 dates without phones**." Khwaaish, filled with joy, responds, "Yes, love, thank you. Let's go and tick off more items from our Wishlist.

Wish #2- Five Weekend Dates without Phones- Completed/Ticked

After that, she says, "I need to leave now; I have a live show tomorrow." Dushyant says, "Just a little while longer, please. Today, I don't feel like letting you go, also don't want to force you to stay. My heart is saying to stop you." She responds, "I need to pack, so I have to go." As she was leaving, Dushyant decided to lighten the moment and recited a poem:

In the moment, you want to depart,

But my heart begs you, "Don't, sweetheart."

Your leaving feels like a poetic crime,

In the verses of love, you're the prime.

Yet, you prepare to say goodbye,

And I'm left with a silent sigh.

In the poetry of love, you're the art,

I'm pleading, "Stay, don't depart."

(This poignant poem captures the emotional struggle of saying goodbye to a loved one. He expresses a heartfelt plea for their departure not to happen, likening it to a poetic crime. Despite the impending farewell, he acknowledges the departing loved one as the prime element in the verses of love. The poem evokes a sense of longing and a silent sigh as the speaker implores the beloved to stay, emphasizing their irreplaceable role in the poetry of love.)

For which she replied

"Oh my! Cheesy Romeo," I would say,

Juliet must go, hit the stage and play.

A promise, my love, we'll meet, no doubt,

In the comedy of life, love's what it's all about."

(The poem playfully acknowledges the romantic connection between her and him, using the characters Romeo and Juliet as a humorous reference. She promises that despite any temporary separation, they will eventually meet again, framing their love story as a delightful comedy within the larger narrative of life.)

After that, he laughed, and they hugged each other tightly and ticked their wish from Wishlist. Yeah, we are progressing **4 wishes** completed from **11 wishes.**

Then, Dushyant booked a cab for her, and then she left. After an hour, Dushyant called her to ask if she had reached home safely, but Khwaaish didn't answer the call. He thought it was unusual because she had never missed his call before. Then he assumed she must have been busy with packing and decided that she would call him later. He went to sleep.

In the midnight, around 2 am, he received a strange call. He picked up and asked who was calling at this late hour. The person on the other end identified himself as a police officer, informing him about a car accident involving the girl he had called last. His heart started racing, and he inquired about the details and her well-being. The police officer urged him to come to the hospital urgently.

Dushyant quickly informed his family at home and Mannat. Mannat said, "You go ahead; I'm also heading there." He rushed out of the house in his night suit and slippers, anxiety gripping his heart.

Panicking, he reached the hospital and spotted Snow. Thoughts raced through his mind as he hoped Snow's presence indicated that Khwaaish's situation wasn't as dire. Anxiously, he approached the reception, urgently inquiring about her whereabouts. The receptionist informed him that she was in the emergency ward and had been taken to the operation theatre. Desperate and concerned, he rushed to the emergency ward, his emotions escalating with each passing moment.

Ten minutes later, Mannat arrived at the hospital. Dushyant, overcome with worry, embraced her tightly, tears streaming down his face. He confessed that he had warned Khwaaish not to go, sensing an ominous intuition. Mannat consoled him and urged patience, assuring him they would hear good news from the doctors soon. They braced themselves, clinging to the hope that she would emerge unscathed from whatever adversity had befallen her.

Medical staff informed him that something really bad happened to Khwaaish. She got into a really bad accident with a huge truck, and it hurt her back and head a lot. The doctors said she needed surgery right away because her injuries were really serious. Dushyant felt super, super worried when he heard this news. It was like a heavy weight of anxiety on his heart. Mannat, saw how upset he was, so she tried to say comforting things to make him feel a little better. She told him that even though things seemed really bad, they could get better. Later, When the doctor emerged from the operation theater, the doctor explained that the current situation is extremely critical, and they are unable to provide specific information at the moment. A surgery has already been performed, and another one is necessary. The doctor emphasized the importance of patience during this challenging time and assured that further updates will be provided as soon as possible.

 After the second surgery, the doctor allowed a short visit with Khwaaish. However, it's essential to note that, given her delicate condition, no conversations were permitted during the visit. The medical team is closely monitoring her recovery, and while physical presence is allowed for a short period, verbal interactions have been restricted to prioritize her well-being and minimize any potential complications.

Khwaaish's parents and Dushyant went to meet her one by one. When Dushyant entered, he couldn't hold back his tears and broke down in front of her. However, she displayed remarkable courage and managed to smile at him. He pleaded, "Please, Tale Teller, don't leave me. I won't be able to live without you.

Please fight, and I promise to make everything right from now onwards. Take care of yourself like you took care of our puppy Snow. We still have to fulfill our Wishlist. How will I complete it alone?" She, too, had tears in her eyes and reassured him, "Don't worry; the Wishlist will be fulfilled." As his allotted time ended, he reluctantly left, glancing at her through a small window. From within, he sensed the gravity of her condition and the slim chance of her survival.

Dushyant returned to Mannat, gripping her arm tightly, and pleaded, "Mannat, do something, please. God, please transfer all her pain and suffering to me and grant her life. " Mannat, too, started crying alongside him. The night seemed endless as they all spent it at the hospital, anxiously awaiting any news about Khwaaish. The heaviness in the air reflected the intensity of their pain and uncertainty.

As the sun rose, Dushyant hurried to her room, his heart filled with worry. Approaching the doctor, he anxiously inquired about her condition. The doctor, with a somber expression, conveyed the heartbreaking news that Khwaaish couldn't be saved. Despite her valiant fight, she succumbed to her injuries. In her final moments, she uttered a poignant word, "Wishlist," expressing a lingering desire.

Dushyant felt as though a thousand needles pierced his chest, the pain unbearable. His entire body trembled, and he staggered away, unable to bear the weight of the tragic reality. Mannat, witnessing the heartbreaking scene, approached the doctor, seeking confirmation. With a somber nod, the doctor confirmed, "She is no more." The realization hit them like a tidal wave, and both Dushyant and Mannat were left shattered, their cries echoing the profound sorrow that had engulfed them. The hospital corridor witnessed an outpouring of grief as they grappled with the inexplicable loss.

Chapter 4- A Grieving Heart and the Call from Fate

The hospital released Khwaaish's lifeless body, and as Dushyant participated in her final rites, he felt an overwhelming wave of despair crashing over him. Memories of their moments together flooded his mind – the poetries, the dates, the dances, their first meeting – creating an unbearable weight on his chest.

The pain he experienced in that moment was unlike anything he had ever felt before. Each memory acted like a dagger, piercing through his heart. Mannat, witnessing Dushyant's agony, couldn't help but feel a deep sympathy for him. Dushyant seemed to have lost all sense of self, as if he had been stripped of his consciousness. The sorrow had consumed him entirely, leaving behind a shell of a man who once knew happiness.

After the cremation, Dushyant locked himself in his room, shutting out the world. Despite Mannat's attempts to reach out through calls and visits, he remained unresponsive. His room became a sanctuary filled with memories – Khwaaish's pictures, the Wishlist board with only four wishes fulfilled out of eleven. Mannat, deeply worried, wanted to help but was at a loss, as Dushyant showed no inclination to accept assistance.

For almost two weeks, Dushyant withdrew from the world, and his parents, too, became increasingly worried about his well-being. Mannat attempted to convey to them that Dushyant and Khwaaish shared a unique and profound connection, surpassing the comprehension of ordinary couples. Their love was beyond the understanding of the world. They communicated without words, understanding each other's needs instinctively. In this state, only Dushyant himself or Khwaaish, who was no longer in this world, could pull him out of this darkness.

Mannat was deeply concerned about Dushyant's condition. He hadn't been answering her calls, and she hadn't seen him for 15 days. His emotional state was troubling, and she couldn't bear to witness him in such distress.

One day, Mannat made a thoughtful decision to bring Snow, the puppy, from Khwaaish's house to Dushyant's place. As Snow joyfully barked, Dushyant, who had isolated himself for a while, opened the door, curious about the commotion. To Mannat's surprise, Dushyant appeared significantly different. He had lost around 12-15 kg, his beard had grown, and he looked like a mere shell of his former self—almost unrecognizable. The impact of grief was evident in his physical transformation.

Witnessing this change, Mannat and Dushyant's parents shared a similar reaction, expressing their concern about what he had done to himself. Mannat then took Snow to Dushyant. Snow, excited to see him, hugged Dushyant and wanted to play. Observing the connection between them, tears welled up in Mannat's eyes. She hugged Dushyant tightly, saying, "My chef friend! Do you know how much Snow and your Noddy missed you? Since Khwaaish left, Snow has been sad for days not eating anything, has given up on playing, and simply sits in a corner, remaining quiet and withdrawn. Today, after so many days, I see Snow so happy. It's the last sign from both of you, and Khwaaish would want to see Snow taken care of well, looking down from above."

Dushyant replied, "I will try for Khwaaish," but Mannat retorted, "You don't have any option, buddy." She instructed him to freshen up and act like his usual self because she had a surprise destination for him. Dushyant asked where, but Mannat refused to disclose it at the moment. Eventually, he got ready, and Mannat took him to Khwaaish's house to meet her parents, who were also concerned about Dushyant.

As they approached her house, Dushyant's legs trembled with hesitation, and he voiced his reluctance, saying, "I'm not sure if I can face this." Mannat, understanding his apprehension, held his hand, providing support. Gathering his courage, they entered her home together. In front of Khwaaish's parents, Dushyant opened up, expressing self-blame, "I feel responsible, Uncle. If I had forcefully stopped Khwaaish, maybe she would still be with us today." Responding with empathy, her parents consoled him, assuring him that there was no fault on his part, and it was a destiny beyond control. They emphasized the importance of moving forward as a collective unit. Despite his initial hesitation, Dushyant agreed, and tears rolled down his cheeks as he had flashbacks.

Dushyant hesitantly entered Khwaaish's room, where the shadows of their past happiness lingered. The room, once filled with laughter and shared dreams, now echoed with the painful silence of her absence. The air seemed heavy with the weight of memories, each corner holding a piece of their intertwined lives.

The room was frozen in time, preserving the essence of Khwaaish's vibrant spirit. Her favorite books lay untouched on the shelf, the pages longing to be turned by the hands that would never touch them again. The soft glow of fairy lights, once a source of warmth, now cast a melancholic hue on the walls.

The bedside table held a collection of trinkets – tokens of their love story. A pair of intertwined bracelets, a dried flower from their date, and a picture frame capturing a moment of sheer joy. The room whispered tales of their laughter, whispered confessions, and the silent promises exchanged in the sanctuary of their shared space. In the corner of the room, a Wishlist board stood as a bittersweet reminder of unfulfilled wishes. Each unchecked wish felt like a dagger, piercing through Dushyant's soul.

Khwaaish's mother approached him and said, "We've kept her room just as she liked it. When we were cleaning, we found these things." Handing Dushyant a collection of Khwaaish's notes, gifts, and memories, she also gave him a canvas of himself with the caption, "My Granny's Mr. Perfect and my Chef," created by her. Mannat gave him a letter, saying aunty found this and it belongs to you and she pass it to him. He opened it and read the contents.

My Dearest Mr. Perfect Chef,

I find it hard to believe that fate could be so kind as to bring someone as wonderful as you into my life. I had almost given up hope that I would find someone who could love me with the same passion and intensity that I had dreamt of since my childhood. It was a dream instilled in me by my dear granny, who always filled my head with tales of true love and prince charming. These stories felt so real to me as a child, and I held onto the belief that such a person would enter my life, sweep me off my feet, and embark on a journey of love.

The letter broke him in tears eventually, Mannat, unable to bear the emotional storm, quietly exited the room, leaving Dushyant to grapple with the harsh reality of a life without Khwaaish. The room, suspended in time, stood as a poignant testimony to a love story that was abruptly and tragically curtailed. It echoed with the remnants of memories, each tear marking the ache of an unfulfilled Wishlist.

Mannat, with a heavy heart, looked at Dushyant and gently uttered, "Life must go on, Dushyant. Khwaaish would never want you to live like this forever. She'll be watching from above, and seeing you in such pain would only make her sad. So, buckle up for her, for the love you shared."

Dushyant, grappling with the reality of his loss, nodded in acknowledgment. He understood that the weight of grief should not shackle him indefinitely. With Mannat's words echoing in his ears, he decided to attempt to integrate himself back into the routine of everyday life. It was a slow process, but he began to find solace in the simple moments and the responsibilities that demanded his attention.

Every day, he would go to work, ensuring Snow, their once-shared companion, received the love and care she deserved. He remained connected with Mannat, finding comfort in their friendship. Taking care of his parents and Khwaaish's parents became an additional responsibility that he willingly embraced. Gradually, he started to comprehend the essence of his newfound roles and responsibilities, accepting them as a part of his journey.

Mannat, although glad to witness Dushyant's efforts to move forward, couldn't help but feel a profound sadness within. She knew that behind the facade of his resilience, he concealed the deep wounds of loss. She understood that Dushyant was attempting to fill the void left by Khwaaish, not with replacements but with responsibilities and connections that required his attention.

Dushyant's daily routine became a manifestation of his acceptance of reality. Yet, every night before going to sleep, he couldn't escape the flood of memories that overwhelmed him.

Khwaaish's absence haunted him, and the void left by her laughter and joy seemed insurmountable. Despite external appearances, Mannat could see that her friend was mourning the loss of more than just a person; he was mourning the loss of a soulmate, a connection that went beyond the tangible.

As he navigated through the rhythm of his life, Dushyant continued to cherish the memories of Khwaaish. He couldn't help but replay the moments they shared, especially during the quiet moments before drifting into slumber. Mannat, being privy to their unique connection, empathized with the struggle he faced each night, yearning for the joyful and cheerful friend who would never return.

In the silent echoes of the night, Dushyant whispered his thoughts to the void, keeping the spirit of Khwaaish alive in his memories.

One day, Dushyant received an unusual call while working in the kitchen, and the True caller displayed "Adoption" on the screen. Initially, he ignored it, but after a couple of hours, curiosity got the better of him, and he decided to answer. On the other end, a girl asked if she was speaking to Mr. Dushyant, and upon confirmation, she explained the reason behind the call.

She informed Dushyant that they had been trying to contact Khwaaish through emails and calls, but her number wasn't reachable and emails were unanswered. It turned out that she had provided Dushyant's alternate contact number, and that's why they were reaching out to him.

Perplexed, Dushyant initially thought it was related to the pet adoption center from where they got Snow. May be call related to Snow's Vaccination. However, the girl on the line surprised him by congratulating him, stating that they were soon to become parents. Dushyant, taken aback, admitted he didn't quite understand. The girl went on to explain that Khwaaish had visited their child adoption center, expressing the desire to adopt a child together. It was a heartfelt wish from both of them.

As the call unfolded, Dushyant found himself grappling with a mixture of shock, surprise, and a profound sense of joy.

In an instant, Dushyant found himself catapulted into a flashback, back to the time when he and Khwaaish were joyfully crafting their Wishlist. He vividly recalled the moment they wrote down their heartfelt desire to welcome a girl child as their first baby. However, at that time, Dushyant was conflicted, grappling with the belief that some things were beyond their control. Khwaaish, with her unwavering optimism, responded to his concerns with the empowering words, "When there is a will, there is a way."

Now, as Dushyant pondered over the mysterious call, he connected the dots. This wasn't just any call; it was **"The call from fate."** The realization hit him like a wave, and he remembered Khwaaish's last words about their Wishlist coming true.

After ending the call with the adoption center, filled with excitement, Dushyant quickly dialed Mannat's number. He urgently requested her to meet him at his place, emphasizing the importance of the news he had to share. Sensing the urgency in his voice, Mannat agreed and suggested he step out of his kitchen as well. Unaware of the impending beautiful transformation in their lives, she prepared to meet Dushyant.

Mannat wasted no time and rushed to Dushyant's home, eager to hear the news he was so excited to share. As he welcomed her into his room, he could barely contain his enthusiasm. He shared with Mannat the surprising call from the adoption center, explaining how Khwaaish had orchestrated everything, leaving them with a sense of fulfillment and completion. Dushyant expressed the belief that Khwaaish's last words were a poignant assurance that their Wishlist would indeed come true.

For the first time since Khwaaish had left, a genuine smile adorned Dushyant's face. Witnessing his happiness, Mannat felt an overwhelming sense of relief and joy. She hugged him tightly, celebrating the newfound hope and positivity that had entered Dushyant's life. Eager to be a part of this journey, she asked when they were going to visit the adoption center. Dushyant, with a newfound happiness, replied, "In two days, Mannat. Please come with me." Mannat readily agreed, sharing in Dushyant's excitement and the promise of a brighter future.

Finally, the day arrived for Dushyant and Mannat to visit the Adoption Center. As they entered the room, a person greeted them, addressing Dushyant and assuming Mannat to be Khwaaish. Dushyant quickly corrected the mistake, explaining that Khwaaish was no longer with them; she had passed away. The person proceeded to discuss the complexities and terms associated with single parenting, expressing the challenges and standards he needed to meet.

Dushyant's excitement had evaporated within the first two minutes of those two days, and a growing sense of disappointment started to show on his face. He felt that this golden opportunity, perhaps the last chance to fulfill Khwaaish's wish, might slip away from his grasp. This was because the adoption center representative explained the challenges of single parenting, emphasizing how it could be demanding for a single individual to take care of a young child and provide the necessary time and attention. On the other hand, Mannat observed Dushyant's reaction and sensed that if this opportunity was missed, he might remain stuck in the same phase and struggle to move forward. As the person continued, Mannat, without second thoughts, interrupted and revealed that they were a couple planning to get married soon. With a firm grip on Dushyant's hand, Mannat confidently asserted that they would jointly raise the child.

Dushyant was taken aback by Mannat's spontaneous revelation, and his surprise was evident. Nonetheless, Mannat's courage and determination to shape their future filled the room. She held Dushyant's hand, not just to keep him silent but to convey their commitment to this new chapter. Addressing the person, she inquired about the next steps and procedures, ready to embrace the challenges and joys that lay ahead.

As they completed all the formalities that day and started to leave the adoption center, Dushyant couldn't hold back his curiosity and asked Mannat why she had claimed they were a couple. He questioned her decision, pointing out that they were friends, not a couple. Mannat, however, stood firm in her choice.

Mannat clarified to Dushyant that when she noticed his saddened expression, a wave of apprehension washed over her. Feeling uncertain about the right course of action, she made a choice that appeared appropriate in that moment. She shared her worry, explaining that if she hadn't taken the initiative, the adoption request might have faced rejection, and his situation might have stayed unchanged. She believed that Khwaaish, looking down from above, would have endorsed her decision.

Dushyant was about to speak, but Mannat insisted that it wasn't about lying; it was about making the right decision. She confessed that she was afraid of wasting Khwaaish's efforts and believed that she might be looking down, saying, "You made the right decision, Mannat." Dushyant, recognizing the depth of Mannat's feelings, remained silent.

As they continued their conversation, Mannat asserted that she wasn't lying. She stated that she can marry him. Dushyant, surprised, mentioned the gravity of marriage and the commitment it required. Mannat, with a genuine smile, assured him that she was returning the favor for all the help he had provided in her life. She acknowledged the uniqueness of his love for Khwaaish, but expressed her readiness to provide a love rooted in friendship that could endure a lifetime if he agreed. In these heartfelt words, Mannat redefined their connection, emphasizing the enduring bond of friendship.

As Dushyant hesitated and asked for some time to think, Mannat gently replied, "Okay, Noddy. I'm scared you might make the wrong choice. Our efforts, (Khwaaish's and mine) should not go to waste."

That night, Dushyant reflected on Mannat's willingness to share her entire life for his small joys, feeling a deep sense of pride for having earned a friend for a lifetime. However, the desire to fulfill Khwaaish's last wish lingered within him.

In the midst of these thoughts, Dushyant immediately called Mannat, expressing, "Mannat, I am sorry, but I can't fulfill Khwaaish's wish at this cost and let your entire life be ruined by my selfish motives." Mannat tried to make him understand, saying, "Dushyant, what do you think? My life will be ruined by marrying you. I know Khwaaish will always have a place in your heart and mind, and I don't intend to take that place. But, remember what she said before leaving you, 'I believe you will definitely fulfill the Wishlist.' Together, we can fulfill her last wish. And I believe you will never ruin my life more than you can provide me with a friendship, love, and respect, the basic needs every girl desire from her partner. These words melted Dushyant's heart, and he asked Mannat, 'Are you sure?' She replied, 'I have the utmost trust in you, Noddy. Go grab this opportunity.''

The next day after work, they met as planned. Dushyant asked Mannat if her family would agree, to which she replied, "Noddy, my family was already suggesting someone like you even before my first marriage. Now, if they find out, they'll be happier than ever." Dushyant chuckled and called her "crazy," to which Mannat responded, "Who knows, Noddy, something has changed in me. I don't know what happened; you've started to look quite good to me. Remember when I jokingly told you about the kind of guy I wanted after my divorce, and I said someone like you, a lively chef? It was a joke back then, but deep down, I secretly hoped to find someone at least 50% like you. But now, it seems I've hit the jackpot with you being a full 100% match." She burst into laughter, and Dushyant felt a profound shift in her, realizing the girl he once considered talkative and immature had matured in a way he hadn't anticipated.

Mannat insisted, "Go and talk to your family instead, find out if they'll accept me as their daughter-in-law." Dushyant agreed, saying, "I'll talk to them today," and she replied, "No, I'm coming with you. I want to stand by your side; you've fought enough battles alone." He smiled and agreed, "Okay, let's eat something first, and then we'll go." Mannat mischievously teased him, saying, "Is today our official date?" Dushyant, with a playful tone, replied, "No, I'm just hungry," and Mannat jokingly said, "Oh, I was just kidding." She then asked him about his food preferences, offering to treat him. Dushyant, smiling, said, "Sure, if you're paying, then the choice is yours." Mannat appreciated his small gestures, saying, "This is your charm; you win hearts with these little things. You know how to treat a woman. I just want to say or it's a request, please bring back my Old Dushyant who was jolly, cheerful and was full of life." He interrupted her, asking which restaurant to go to, and She teases him with playful banter and provides guidance to help him along the way. They headed to the restaurant and enjoyed their meal together.

After dinner, feeling a bit anxious, they proceeded to Dushyant's house to address the situation with his parents. Mannat, sensing his nervousness, held his hand for reassurance and comfort. Together, they explained the entire situation to his father, discussing the matter openly and honestly. His father engaged in a heated argument, expressing disapproval of fulfilling what he deemed as trivial wishes from Khwaaish's Wishlist. Mannat interrupted to address his father, saying,

"Uncle, I know this might seem childish to you, but Khwaaish considered you her father and you treated her like a daughter. I am just like your daughter. While it might seem childish to you, if you set aside societal norms and think with an open heart, you'll realize that these joys are a blessing from Universe, something Dushyant himself did not invite but received in contrary. Moreover, it was Khwaaish's last wish. Please reconsider."

However, his father remained adamant, citing inter-caste marriage as acceptable but objecting to a union with a divorcee. Dushyant pleaded, "Even God fulfills the last wish of a dying person. Please, you are still a human being." His father disagreed, maintaining that he couldn't give their family surname to Mannat. In response, Dushyant angrily proposed, "Okay, don't give her our family surname. I can take her family surname instead." Upon hearing this, Mannat turned her gaze towards Dushyant, contemplating the words he had just spoken and what kind of a beautiful soul he was. He was willing to break stereotypes and take her family surname, a gesture that touched her deeply. In that moment, Mannat felt a fleeting but intense connection, giving her heart to Dushyant momentarily. She felt blessed, realizing that the person she had been searching for all her life was right in front of her.

His father grudgingly agreed, saying, "Okay, take it and don't talk to me after this. Leave this house as soon as possible. Our family doesn't deserve a girl like her." In response, Dushyant took a stand for Mannat, asserting, "Don't disrespect her. You have always disrespected my mother, and I never argued. But now, she is going to be my wife. I am sorry, Mom; I could never stand up for you before, but today, I cannot do that. Mannat deserves as much respect as any normal person."

With a farewell to his mother, Dushyant took Mannat's hand, and they left. Mannat, in her heart, fell in love with him even more for the way he stood up for her in front of her own father. However, she advised him not to disrespect his father. Dushyant clarified, "I am not disrespecting him. He has a traditional mindset that, as a man, my decisions will prevail in this house. It was high time to bring them out of this misconception."

Sitting in the car, Dushyant was visibly disappointed and disturbed after the argument with his father. Suddenly, Mannat kissed him on the cheek and said, "Thank you, Noddy. No one has ever done something like this for me. I have been humiliated and abused, but I couldn't take a stand for myself. Today, you proved that a guy like you is not one in millions but a once-in-a-lifetime soul. Do you really want to take my family surname?" She smiled as she lightened his mood and he said, "Now I don't have any choice. I gave my verdict in court, and I can't back off." She replied, "Aww! Thank you." He dropped her off at her house, and Mannat asked where he would go at this late hour as he left his home after argument. He mentioned checking into a hotel, but she insisted he come to her house for the night. He hesitated, saying he couldn't bother her, but she took his car keys and said, "Come quietly."

Upon reaching Mannat's house, Dushyant noticed her cat, Martha, and commented on how much she had grown. Mannat replied, "Yes, she had no other option." She told him to freshen up while she made coffee. After freshen up and they both sat near balcony, while sipping coffee, Mannat asked about his plans. Dushyant shared that he would buy a house using his savings as down payments and applying for a home loan for rest of the amount. Although he had saved this money for opening his cloud kitchen in the future, he now considered it a basic requirement. He explained, "When we get married, we need a house for all of us – Snow, Martha, you, me, and the unnamed adopted child. We need our space." Mannat hugged him, acknowledging that Khwaaish was right about him – his heart was as pure as gold. She expressed her realization that Khwaaish told her once he would go to any limit for his loved ones, and she appreciated his honesty, knowing he would always speak the truth.

Mannat found herself growing more emotionally attached to Dushyant. There was a shift in the way she perceived him, and she began to notice qualities that went beyond their friendship. Her feelings for him were evolving into something deeper, a romantic connection she hadn't anticipated. Despite these emotions, Mannat was acutely aware of the unique bond Dushyant shared with Khwaaish. She understood that if, by some miracle, Khwaaish were to return and he had to choose between them, Dushyant would undoubtedly opt for Khwaaish. However, she found solace in the honesty and integrity that defined Dushyant's character. She appreciated that he would never betray their friendship, always staying true to his feelings and commitments.

In a span of just one week, Dushyant managed to secure a new house, making the initial payment. However, there was a slight delay in gaining possession as some essential renovations were still underway. Amidst these changes, an unexpected strain surfaced in Dushyant's relationship with his father. The once open line of communication now seemed closed, adding an extra layer of tension to an already complex situation. As proceeded with their plan to adopt a child, they encountered a legal requirement. To fulfill the necessary procedures for adoption, Mannat and Dushyant needed to formalize their relationship through marriage. This step was crucial as marriage documents played a pivotal role in the adoption process, prompting them to take this significant step in their journey toward parenthood.

Dushyant deep down thought that Mannat had dedicated her life selflessly to fulfilling his and Khwaaish's wishes. Now, she deserved special treatment and care. With this in mind, he planned a date for Mannat. Renting a special space, he texted her, "Are you ready for our first official date tonight?" Mannat looked at her phone, beaming with surprising joy, and replied, "Yes, I am ready. Text me the time and place." Dushyant assured her, "Don't worry, just be ready. I'll pick you up from your home." Throughout the day, Mannat remained happy, eagerly anticipating what the evening would hold.

Dushyant, the chef, wanted to make a memorable evening for Mannat, so he carefully selected a picturesque rooftop adorned with fairy lights, setting a romantic table for just the two of them. As he strummed the guitar and recited heartfelt poetry, Mannat sensed a shift in his mood. Dushyant, known for effortlessly weaving poetic verses, unexpectedly halted, his emotions stirred by memories of Khwaaish – the last person he had loved, who was now no longer a part of their world. The weight of the past cast a bittersweet shadow over the otherwise enchanting date.

Sensing his distress, Mannat gently reached out and held his hand. She spoke comforting words, assuring him that it was okay to feel the pain and offering a listening ear whenever he needed. Dushyant appreciated her understanding, and as the evening continued, he mustered the courage to proceed with the date. He continued with his poetry.

Mannat, I never knew my best friend would become my life's delight,

Through thick and thin, you stood by me, a constant shining light.

The journey from best friend to life partner is quite rare,

You've carved a special place in my heart, beyond compare.

In the moments we've shared, a world of sweetness resides,

You've created a space within me where love and joy abides.

The decision to fulfill a Wishlist has led me to this day,

Mannat, will you be the one with whom I'll forever stay?

No ordinary person can make such a choice,

You're extraordinary, Mannat, with a unique voice.

The time has come to make you a permanent part,

To walk together in this journey, no backing off, no depart.

Think about this night, a moment of love so grand,

This is our chance to create a story, hand in hand.

With you, my dear, there'll be no end in sight,

Mannat, become my life partner, embrace this night.

(In this heartfelt poetry, Dushyant expresses his deep appreciation for Mannat, acknowledging her unwavering support and the special place she holds in his heart. He reflects on their journey from best friends to a rare connection as life partners. Dushyant, prompted by the desire to fulfill a Wishlist, pops the question, asking Mannat to be his forever. He emphasizes her uniqueness and the extraordinary nature of their bond, inviting her to join him on this journey without hesitation. The poem is a declaration of love and a proposal for a lifelong commitment.)

Mannat felt with waves of emotion in herself. For the grand finale, Dushyant, in his role as a chef, had prepared a special dish. As Mannat opened the lid, a tantalizing aroma filled the air. To her surprise, she found a carefully crafted message written on curry with white cream, "Will you marry me, Mannat?" with the same ring which he purchased for Khwaaish with Mannat but he never got the chance to give it to her. Dushyant stood there, a mix of nervousness and hope in his eyes, waiting for her response.

Touched by the depth of Dushyant's emotions and the unique proposal, Mannat felt a surge of overwhelming feelings. As she looked at Dushyant, who had poured his heart out in a truly memorable manner, tears of joy filled her eyes. With a nod and a heartfelt "Yes," Mannat accepted Dushyant's proposal to marry him. The rooftop setting transformed into a witness to this beautiful moment, symbolizing the triumph of love over past sorrows and marking the beginning of a new chapter in the journey of Dushyant and Mannat.

Mannat's eyes sparkled with tears, accompanied by a radiant smile. She gently kissed Dushyant on the forehead, expressing her heartfelt thanks. "I'll never let you down, Noddy. You bring so much brightness into my life," she said.

In response, Dushyant smiled, genuinely grateful. "Thank you, Mannat, for trusting me. It means a lot," he replied.

As their date came to an end, he dropped her off at her home. Mannat found it hard to sleep that night, the memories of their enchanting time together replaying in her mind. She couldn't help but reflect on how she had never experienced such complete and thoughtful treatment before.

The warmth of Dushyant's gestures lingered, leaving a profound impact on Mannat. Love and joy were intricately woven into the fabric of her heart.

As each day unfolded, Mannat found her feelings for Dushyant growing deeper. With her naturally talkative and open-hearted nature, she shared everything like a chatterbox. Their bond steadily became stronger, leaning more towards love than just friendship. In essence, Mannat had wholeheartedly given her heart and soul to Dushyant.

After a span of days, the much-anticipated wedding day of Mannat and Dushyant finally arrived, and the couple eagerly entered the courtroom for their marriage ceremony. Mannat's parents stood as witnesses from her side, while Dushyant's mother supported him as witness. She was excited to marry him.

As the intricate process of verifying identity documents commenced, Mannat's heart skipped a beat when she noticed something extraordinary. To her surprise and overwhelming emotion, Dushyant had officially adopted her family surname. A rush of gratitude and disbelief surged through Mannat as she locked eyes with Dushyant, realizing the profound significance of his actions. In a hushed yet emotionally charged voice, she whispered, "You weren't joking about adopting my surname, were you?" Dushyant, with a tender replied, "No, I told you before, it's not a big deal." Mannat, moved beyond words, couldn't hold back the tears that welled up in her eyes.

"Today, you've given me the most beautiful wedding gift, something I will cherish until my last breath," Mannat expressed with a mixture of awe and gratitude. Overwhelmed by the depth of his gesture, she added, "I must be the first woman whose husband chose her family surname."

In that moment, Mannat's heart melted, and she sat down with joy, tears of happiness streaming down her face. "I love you so much, and I promise to love you each day with the same passion," she declared. Dushyant, standing beside her, strengthened his commitment by saying, "I told you I would stick to my words. This is one of the pieces of evidence." Mannat smiled and affirmed her belief in his promises, holding his hand.

Dushyant's mother, witnessing this beautiful exchange, couldn't hold back her emotions. She spoke to her son with pride, "I am so proud of you today for what you've done. Every mother deserves a son like you, who respects everyone so humbly. Thank you for choosing me as your mother." She hugged Dushyant, who was now emotional, and blessed him, encouraging him to fulfill all his wishes. The ceremony continued, marking the beginning of a new chapter in Mannat and Dushyant's journey together.

They both shifted to their new, beautiful house, which Dushyant had purchased earlier but decided to enter his sweet home on the wedding day.

The next day, Dushyant excitedly told Mannat, "Please, let's go to the adoption center. We need to submit our marriage documents." Mannat replied, "Which documents? I don't need to submit any documents; I'm not interested in fulfilling Khwaaish's Wishlist." Dushyant was shocked and felt betrayed, as he thought she had used him to get married.

After a pause, Mannat revealed, "How did you like my joke?" and burst into laughter. Seeing Dushyant's eyes welling up with tears, she quickly hugged him and said, "I'm just playing a prank. I'm sorry." She wiped away his tears, kissed him, and reassured him that it was all in good fun. Dushyant said, "Mannat, there's a limit to jokes, and you almost scared the life out of me. Please don't do something like that again." She apologized, then urged him, "Come on, let's go to the adoption center, and afterward, we can tidy up the house. Everything is scattered here and there." They both left to center.

With the formalities of document submission completed, Mannat and Dushyant found themselves in a state of eager expectation, their hearts brimming with anticipation for the call that would herald the next chapter of their lives as parents.

As they waited for the adoption center's signal to bring their child home, the couple immersed themselves in the task of transforming their living space into a haven of love and warmth. Each corner of the house echoed with the whispers of excitement and joy, as they carefully arranged and adorned the rooms in anticipation of the tiny footsteps that would soon grace their home.

Amidst the flurry of activity, Dushyant's gaze fell upon a framed photograph on the wall, capturing the radiant smile of Khwaaish. A momentary hesitation lingered in his heart, a concern that perhaps Mannat might find it uncomfortable to have a constant reminder of his late love. Sensing his unspoken thoughts, Mannat approached him, her eyes catching the direction of his gaze.

Without a word, she playfully hung a thread between two hooks on the wall, bridging the gap between Khwaaish's photo and the rest of the adorned space. Her gesture spoke volumes – a silent acknowledgment of the bond they all shared. In that moment, Mannat's eyes conveyed a depth of understanding, assuring Dushyant that she cherished the connection that tied them all together.

Addressing his unspoken concerns, Mannat spoke, "I know what you're thinking, that I wouldn't like you reminiscing about Khwaaish even now. But my dear husband, she is the thread that binds us. She is the reason we are each other. We had forgotten how to live, and she gave us the purpose to do so. She was my friend, and I learned the essence of friendship from her. How could I forget her, or let you forget her? She is a part of us, and I wouldn't have it any other way."

Dushyant, moved by Mannat's maturity and profound understanding, found himself enchanted by the jhalli (carefree) spirit that she embodied. In that shared laughter, they paid a silent tribute to Khwaaish, expressing their gratitude for the role she played in shaping their lives and bringing them together. The thread hung delicately, symbolizing the intricate connection between past, present, and future – a visual testament to the enduring power of love and friendship that would carry them through the beautiful journey of parenthood that awaited them.

As Mannat stood there, gazing at the Wishlist board, she felt an overwhelming surge of emotions. Dushyant, too, was caught off guard by the revelation. "We didn't even realize," he murmured in astonishment. Mannat, with a soft smile, replied, "Indeed, we didn't orchestrate this; it's Khwaaish who worked her magic through us. It's like she is writing our story from the heavens, and the universe is aligning everything in the best way possible."

"There's something about you," Mannat continued, "that Khwaaish saw even in her final moments. That unwavering trust she had in you when she said, 'I believe you will fulfill the Wishlist.' I am immensely proud of you, and I also consider myself incredibly fortunate that she chose me to be part of this noble cause. In her eyes, we were the ones she had the utmost

faith in, above all in this world. I believe her benevolent spirit
will continue guiding us in the days to come. Mark my words,
she will keep helping us in her own way."

The air in the room felt charged with a mix of gratitude,
reverence, and a sense of destiny being carefully woven by
unseen hands. As they reflected on the profound impact of
Khwaaish's wishes, Mannat and Dushyant found solace in the
belief that her spirit would forever be a guiding force in their
journey.

Chapter 5- Rebirth and New Beginnings

Mannat stood before the Wishlist board, a visual diary of dreams that had become intertwined with the tapestry of their shared journey. With a mischievous grin, she called out to Dushyant again, "Hey Noddy, come here, I want to show you something." Intrigued, he walked over, asking, "What is it?"

She pointed to the Wishlist; her eyes gleaming with excitement. "You know, we were working on fulfilling one of these wishes together, and, unknowingly, you've managed to check off not just one but four wishes!" Dushyant's eyes widened, and he said, "Really? Which ones?" Mannat began unraveling the delightful surprises.

"Wish #6 - Propose each other in a Unique way for Marriage," Mannat declared, her eyes sparkling with revelation. Dushyant's eyebrows shot up in disbelief. "Are you serious?" he exclaimed. She nodded, recounting the curry proposal, which, unbeknownst to them, had become a unique and cherished memory.

Moving on, Mannat continued, **"Wish #9** - Having a Cat and Dog as Pets." A warmth filled the room as Dushyant realized the subtle fulfillment of this wish in the form of Snow and Martha, their furry companions who had brought immeasurable joy to their lives.

Her finger traced the lines of the Wishlist, reaching **"Wish #5 -** Taking the Girl's Surname after Marriage." Mannat looked into Dushyant's eyes, emphasizing the profound significance of him embracing her family surname. His heart swelled with pride and love, understanding the depth of that simple yet significant act.

Finally, they arrived at **"Wish #8** - Own a Dream House." Mannat's words echoed with a touch of awe and gratitude. "You bought this house independently without anyone's help. This, my dear Noddy, is nothing short of a miracle."

Dushyant was astounded, his eyes reflecting a mix of disbelief and joy. Mannat continued, "Our life is turning into a fairy tale, and these wishes have become the magical threads holding us together. It's like Khwaaish orchestrated this miracle for us." They stood there, basking in the realization that the wishes on that board had not only been fulfilled but had also transformed their lives in ways they hadn't imagined.

That day held profound significance for both of them as Khwaaish's Wishlist was gradually, almost unknowingly, getting fulfilled, and they hadn't even realized it. Dushyant told Mannat, "Mannat, you understand me from within. I might not be able to give you the same love that I felt for Khwaaish. But from today onwards, I promise that I will try my best to love you more than Khwaaish. Your heart is large and pure. What you've done for me, I probably wouldn't have been able to do if I were in your place. But hearing this, Mannat became emotional and said, "Dushyant, you've said enough. What you've expressed is more than sufficient for me. But I want to confess to you that I have fallen deeply in love with you. My heart is captivated, and I see a light in you that can illuminate anyone from within. Do you remember when you first met Khwaaish, you mended her broken world from within. You alleviated her pain by giving her just one thing – your true love. You've also taught me how to live. Before this, I was never this happy in life."

Now Wishes below were granted simultaneously, unfolding like a magical spectacle.

Wish #5- Taking the Girl's Surname after Marriage- Completed

Wish #6- Propose in a Unique way for Marriage- Completed

Wish #8- Own Dream House- Completed

Wish #9- Having a Cat and Dog as Pets- Completed

The next day was a unique Sunday for Mannat. When she woke up, she was pleasantly surprised. Chef Dushyant had gone out of his way to make her a wonderful bed coffee and her breakfast. He prepared a mouthwatering "Gourmet Avocado Toast with Poached Eggs and Smoked Salmon." This exquisite dish would feature perfectly toasted artisanal bread topped with creamy avocado mash, poached eggs with runny yolks, and a generous serving of premium smoked salmon. Garnished with fresh herbs, a drizzle of olive oil, and a sprinkle of cracked black pepper.

The way he prepared it showed so much care and attention that Mannat felt torn between enjoying the delicious meal and wanting to keep it looking beautiful. She couldn't resist capturing the special moment and shared a photo on Instagram with the caption, "Special treatment received from an extra special person," tagged Dushyant.

Dushyant then entered the room, saying, "Oh my dear dove, you're awake. I prepared breakfast. Quickly eat it; otherwise, it will get cold. Today, I need your time, and I'm taking you somewhere special." Mannat responded playfully, "What's this talk about time, sir? Claim my life; I'm at your service." He chuckled, "Shut up and eat this. We have to go somewhere. It's a surprise."

Mannat spoke, "You should have woken me up earlier." He replied, "No, when you were sleeping, there was a peace and a smile on your face, and I have no right to take that away from you."

Mannat teased him, "Oh, these cheesy lines of yours will make me your crazy fan, my Romeo." Dushyant just smiled and said, "Okay, just get ready fast. We don't have much time." She hugged him, kissed him on the forehead and thanked him for breakfast, and said, "Give me half an hour." He agreed, "Okay, take your time."

When she emerged after half an hour, Dushyant couldn't help but compliment her, "Someone is looking beautiful today." Mannat cheekily replied, "Well, when your husband is this handsome, you've got to match his level." She then asked about Snow and Martha, their pets, and Dushyant assured her that he had dropped them off at her parents' house.

Excitement filled the air as Mannat realized that today was going to be a special day, possibly a date. Dushyant's smile confirmed it, and Mannat's eyes sparkled with joy.

On this special date, Dushyant took Mannat down memory lane, back to the place where their beautiful journey from friendship to life partners began – their college. The college, situated in the heart of Delhi, was the witness to their laughter, shared secrets, and the blossoming of an extraordinary connection.

Their first stop was the college canteen, the hub of their initial interactions. Dushyant pointed to the corner table where they had their first conversation. Mannat chuckled, remembering how Dushyant had tried to impress her with his not-so-impressive culinary skills by making a cup of coffee that was more sugar than caffeine.

As they strolled through the campus, they reached the spot where Dushyant had first played the guitar for Mannat. Recreating the magic, he strummed a few chords, and they found themselves lost in the melody of their favorite friendship songs.

The library, where they had spent countless hours studying together (or at least attempting to), brought back a wave of nostalgia. Mannat teased Dushyant about his habit of reciting poetry to attract girls' attention during study breaks. He recited his first poetry again on their friendship and asked her if she remembered it now. Title of the Poem "I found a Friend for Life".

In the midst of textbooks and academic strife,

I discovered a new lease on life.

Amidst the notes and the endless chatter,

I found a friend whose bond would only matter.

"I found a friend for life," I would say with pride,

In the library where dreams and ambitions reside.

With every rhyme and every poetic line,

A friendship blossomed, truly divine.

In study breaks, with books set aside,

I, the newbie poet, took in stride.

I penned verses about laughter and shared dreams,

About friendship's glow and supportive schemes.

"Amidst the pages of academic lore,

I found a friend worth so much more.

In the echoes of our laughter and the shared delight,

I discovered a bond, strong and bright."

Our friendship, a poem written in fate,

A melody that even time couldn't abate.

In those verses, penned with ink so true,

The seeds of a friendship forever grew.

So, in the college's poetic embrace,

I found solace and a special place.

"I found a friend for life," he proclaimed,

In the verses of a friendship, untamed.

(The poem talks about finding a special friend during the challenges of college life. Despite the stress of academics, the narrator discovers a valuable friendship that goes beyond just studying. They express joy in sharing laughter, dreams, and support during breaks from studies. The verses describe this friendship as a beautiful and enduring connection, like a poem written by fate. Overall, the poem celebrates the unique bond formed in the midst of academic pursuits and declares the discovery of a lifelong friend.)

As Mannat teased Dushyant about his early attempts at poetry during their college days, he couldn't help but smile at the playful banter. She jokingly questioned whether he still remembered his first attempt at a poem, especially one centered around their blossoming friendship. Mannat, overwhelmed with nostalgia, couldn't hold back the emotional twinkle in her eyes. The words might have been amateurish, but they were a testament to the beginning of a beautiful friendship that had now transformed into a lifelong connection.

Their last stop was the college terrace, the place where they had shared dreams and aspirations under the open sky. The sun began to set, casting a warm glow on the campus. Dushyant looked into Mannat's eyes and said, "This is where it all began, and here we are – from best friends to life partners."

As they enjoyed the breathtaking view, Dushyant whispered sweet promises, and Mannat felt a profound connection between their past, present, and the promising future ahead. The date was a perfect blend of laughter, love, and the joy of reminiscing about the beautiful journey they had embarked on together.

In the quiet moments after their special date, Mannat couldn't contain the overwhelming emotions that swirled within her. Turning to Dushyant, she spoke from the depths of her heart, "You're the best, Noddy. I feel incredibly lucky to have you in my life. This is the best anyone could ever do for their wife. Thank you, my husband."

With those words, she wrapped her arms around him in a warm embrace, expressing a love that transcended the ordinary. As she closed her eyes, a silent prayer of gratitude echoed in her heart, thanking the stars above for bringing such a kind and wonderful person into her life.

After a period of eager anticipation, the adoption center finally called to deliver the heartwarming news – Congratulations Mannat and Dushyant you both become parents. Having successfully navigated through all the terms and legalities, this moment was filled with emotions, especially for Dushyant. However, words seemed to elude him, and his eyes spoke volumes.

Seeing the myriad emotions in Dushyant's eyes, Mannat comforted him with understanding words, "I can feel what you're going through." Together, they proceeded to the adoption center to welcome the child into their lives.

Upon reaching the center, Dushyant was visibly nervous. Mannat, perceptive as always, could sense the turmoil in his heart. Trying to ease his anxiety, she reassured him, "Don't worry; it'll be a girl." The moment these words reached Dushyant, tears welled up in his eyes. Mannat, without uttering a single word, had already conveyed her understanding of his unspoken emotions.

As they stepped into the adoption center, Dushyant couldn't help but express the overwhelming emotions that surged within him. He turned to Mannat and uttered, "I can't help but feel like I'm going through labor pains, akin to what women endure during childbirth." Mannat, touched by his honesty and vulnerability, gently responded, "You're such a pure and sensitive soul," as she intertwined her fingers with his and placed their hands over her heart.

The officials at the adoption center presented the child to the couple. It was an incredibly poignant moment that brought tears of joy and an indescribable sense of fulfillment to Dushyant and Mannat. The child they had been patiently waiting for was a "Girl", and the emotional weight of the moment rendered them speechless.

Dushyant, in awe, examined every delicate feature of the baby – from her tiny eyes to her button-like nose, from her cherubic lips to her adorable ears. In those innocent features, he saw a poignant reflection of Khwaaish, the guiding force that had brought them to this point. The baby, unaware of the emotional journey unfolding before her, responded with joyous laughter, filling the room with a sweetness that only children possess.

Overwhelmed by the depth of the moment, Dushyant whispered to Mannat, "Look at her. Every feature resembles Khwaaish. It feels as though she has returned to my life." Mannat, her eyes brimming with both tears and joy, nodded in agreement, "Yes, indeed she's back and this feels like her last gift to us as a tribute."

The couple found themselves in a silent embrace, their tears becoming a testament to the profound emotions that the arrival of this child had stirred within them.

Dushyant, overwhelmed with joy, turned to Mannat and expressed, "Today, I've received the greatest happiness the world has to offer. We'll give this child a name that resonates uniquely." Mannat, feeling the presence of Khwaaish in this moment, remarked, "I can sense a glimpse of Khwaaish in her. It feels as if she has taken rebirth. Let's name her 'Khaawish' because after all, the essence of her is fulfilled wishes, and ours has come true."

The atmosphere was charged with emotion as Dushyant, gazing at Mannat, whispered, "Khaawish," tears streaming down his face. He nodded, confirming, "Yes, let's name her Khaawish." In that tender moment, they decided to bestow upon their child the name that symbolized not only their deepest desires but also the beautiful connection they shared with Khwaaish. And thus, their baby girl, a manifestation of love and wishes fulfilled, was named Khaawish – a living embodiment of the extraordinary journey that brought Dushyant and Mannat together.

Bringing baby Khaawish to their dream home, Dushyant and Mannat decided to mark the joyous occasion by imprinting the baby's footprints on the wall with Kumkum—a symbol of auspicious beginnings. The announcement of their new family member echoed in their home, and both sets of parents arrived to celebrate this momentous occasion.

Dushyant was taken aback when he saw his father entering his own home. The unexpected visit left him speechless, and as his father embraced him, expressing remorse for his previous actions, Dushyant was overwhelmed with gratitude. Mannat's intervention had not only bridged the gap but had also mended a long-standing misunderstanding between father and son.

In a lighthearted moment, Dushyant questioned how this miracle had occurred—how "Gabbar Singh" transformed into "Alok Nath" in a united family with funny reference in context with Bollywood characters. Mannat playfully acknowledged her own talents, suggesting that she, too, possessed the skills to convince even the most resistant individuals. She shared her heartfelt conversation with Dushyant's father, revealing the countless ways he had contributed selflessly to others and emphasizing his continued commitment to spreading love.

Adding a touch of humor, Mannat playfully expressed her fear of receiving less love from Dushyant now that his love seemed to be distributed to everyone—his parents, her parents, Snow, Martha, and now baby Khaawish. Dushyant reassured her that their collective love would surround her, making it impossible for her to feel neglected. Mannat, teasing him about his overflowing affection, wondered where he managed to find so much love. Dushyant, with a smile, simply replied, "Never underestimate the power of love. We all—my parents, your parents, Snow, Martha, baby Khaawish, and me—will shower you with so much love that you won't know how to handle it."

Mannat, impressed yet again, quipped about his cheesy yet heartwarming gestures, expressing her disbelief at his ability to turn the tables whenever she thought she had him beaten. Their banter continued, creating a loving atmosphere in their home, where each member was a testament to the power of love and understanding.

In the midst of welcoming baby Khaawish to their family, Dushyant and Mannat decided to perform a ritual to solidify the bonds of love and acceptance within their home. As they went through the customs, Mannat observed the genuine emotions surfacing in Dushyant's father. The ritual held a special significance, not only for the newborn but also for the entire family.

Dushyant's father, while witnessing the ceremony, couldn't help but get emotional. The sight of his house, now transformed into a sanctuary of love and unity, stirred unexpected feelings within him. Approaching Dushyant, he uttered words that were more powerful than anyone could have anticipated. "I am proud of you, my son."

These simple yet profound words struck a chord deep within Dushyant's heart. It was an acknowledgment he hadn't expected, a validation of his choices and efforts. The emotional resonance of those words reflected the unspoken desire for acceptance and pride that every child harbor in their relationship with their parents. In that moment, the house echoed with sentiments of love, forgiveness, and a newfound understanding that had finally taken root in their family.

Today, the most hard-fought wish, for which Dushyant and Mannat dedicated extensive effort, has finally materialized. They have evolved from being friends bound by friendship to becoming life partners in the sacred bond of marriage. Both of them, along with their baby Khwaaish, joyfully marked this accomplishment by ticking off that cherished wish on their wish list board.

Wish #3- Wish to have a First child as a girl – completed

Now, Dushyant dedicates all his quality time to his small family, ensuring the well-being of Baby Khwaaish with utmost care and affection. Mannat marvels at how he provides even more love than she could have imagined, taking care of every aspect of Baby Khwaaish's life. Dushyant actively engages in tasks such as feeding, changing diapers, and checking on the baby every hour throughout the night, even if he himself sleeps for only 4-5 hours. Mannat appreciates how he goes above and beyond to care for all of them, a level of dedication she believes no one else in the world can match. In her eyes, Dushyant is not just a better partner, but also an unparalleled father to Snow, Martha, and Baby Khwaaish, creating a beautiful and small world that revolves around their happiness

However, deep down, Mannat felt a twinge of sadness for Dushyant because he had put his dream of opening his cloud kitchen on the back burner to ensure everyone's happiness. She had known since their college days that he harbored the dream of having his own cloud kitchen. Despite being a chef, he had invested all his savings in building a home, prioritizing his family's well-being over his own aspirations.

In a poignant moment, Mannat sweetly hugged him from behind and whispered, "Hey, my forever love! Can I ask you for a favor? I have a small wish. Can you add it to Wishlist Board?"

Dushyant responded with warmth, "Of course, tell me, and if it's within my reach, I'll do my best to fulfill it." Mannat assured him, "I have complete faith in you; you can make it happen." She then opened up about her wish, "Open your own cloud kitchen now; it's been delayed for too long. I know it's been your dream since college, and it's also one of my wishes."

Dushyant, with a gentle smile, explained the financial constraints, saying, "I wish I could fulfill it now, but due to lack of funds, I can't. I invested my money in buying this house." Mannat, undeterred, sweetly understood, "I knew we would have to wait, but I have some savings, and if you need more, I can take a loan for your dream." Dushyant hesitated, saying he couldn't take the money, and Mannat insisted, "It's our money, and we're one, if not in person, then in identity." Dushyant, expressing his reluctance, stated that he couldn't accept her hard-earned money. She responded, "Consider it a gift from me; please take the money. Okay, here's an idea – give me equity in your business, like they do on Shark Tank." He laughed, and she pleaded with him, saying, "Please, Noddy! Go fulfill my wish and your dreams. This is the first and last time I'm asking you for something." Eventually, he agreed. Mannat then said, "See, my talent. I convinced your father with the same charm." She laughed, kissed him, and said, "Thank you for considering my request."

Dushyant was deeply moved by her words, realizing the immense amount of trust she had in him. He then said, "But before that, we have to fulfill a wish from the Wishlist. So, are you ready, my partner?" To this, she replied confidently, "I'm born ready! Tell me what we need to do." Dushyant explained that they had to create a post-wedding video script and shoot it. Upon hearing this, Mannat became excited, realizing that it was

Khwaaish's wish. Dushyant gently tapped her forehead, remarking, "And Baby Khwaaish is back in our life as well." Mannat pulled his cheeks and said, "Every day, I am falling more and more in love with you," to which he responded, "Same here. So, shall we start planning?" Mannat enthusiastically replied, "Yes, of course!"

Chapter 6- Fulfillment of Wishes and Happy Endings?

Following that, Dushyant and Mannat enthusiastically immersed themselves in the creative process of preparing for their post-wedding video. In a collaborative spirit, they decided to allocate a generous week's time, allowing each other the space to pen down their individual ideas. Dushyant proposed, "Take this week to write down your thoughts, and I'll do the same. Afterward, we can combine our ideas and see what kind of output we come up with."

After the designated week elapsed, both eagerly shared their written musings with one another. A symphony of laughter and camaraderie echoed as they playfully reviewed and critiqued each other's ideas, approving some while disapproving others. Through this collaborative process, they carefully molded and refined their creative vision, ultimately resulting in the formulation of a well-crafted script.

Now armed with a script that mirrored the essence of their love story, they transitioned to the exciting phase of video production. The camera, a silent witness to their unfolding journey, was brought into play, capturing the candid moments that encapsulated the essence of their post-wedding bliss.

The completion of their post-wedding video became a month-long adventure for Dushyant and Mannat. Amidst this creative journey, they added a touch of spontaneity by taking a vacation dedicated to capturing picturesque moments. Carefully selecting diverse and charming locations in different towns, they utilized the backdrop to tell their love story visually. The camera documented every laugh, embrace, and shared glance, turning their vacation into an integral part of the video's narrative. This month-long endeavor not only crafted a beautiful visual story but also allowed them to create lasting memories in various scenic settings.

Here is the culmination of their dedicated efforts—a final video output that beautifully encapsulates the depth of their love story. Every frame, moment, and shared glance within the video serves as a testament to their genuine bond, creating a heartfelt narrative that resonates with joy, laughter, and togetherness. This visual masterpiece not only tells their unique tale but also captures the essence of their journey, offering a glimpse into the warmth and authenticity of their relationship.

Title: "A Journey of Love: Our Post-Wedding Adventure"

[Opening Scene]

Dushyant and Mannat stand hand in hand, smiling at the camera.

Mannat: (with excitement) Hey, everyone! It's us, Mannat, and Dushyant. And guess what? We're officially married!

Dushyant: (grinning) That's right! Today, we're taking you on an extraordinary journey through our post-wedding adventures, a tale woven with threads of love, laughter, and a few surprises along the way.

[Scene 1 - Love Chronicles]

Soft romantic music playing in the background.

Mannat: (gazing at Dushyant) From being friends to life partners, our love story has been nothing short of a fairy tale.

Dushyant: (looking at Mannat) Absolutely. And to think it all started in college with me reciting cheesy poetry to get attention.

Mannat: (laughs) Oh, those poetry days! Our love for friendship blossomed like the most beautiful sonnet.

[Scene 2 - A Dash of Comedy]

Dushyant attempting to cook with an apron that says "Chef in Love."

Dushyant: (smiling awkwardly) So, I thought I'd surprise Mannat by cooking her favorite dish. Let's just say, my apron is the only thing in love here.

Mannat: (laughing) Bless his heart, he tried! Who knew laughter and love could be the perfect recipe?

[Scene 3 - Travel Diaries]

Montage of Dushyant and Mannat exploring different corners of the city.

Mannat: (excitedly) One of the best parts of our journey is exploring new places together. Whether it's the serene beaches or bustling city streets, every moment is special.

Dushyant: (looking at Mannat) And I promise, Mannat, there are many more adventures to come. Our passports might run out of pages in future, but our love story is just beginning.

[Scene 4 - Emotional Moments]

Mannat holding back tears.

Mannat: (emotionally) Life is a rollercoaster, and we've faced our share of ups and downs. But together, we've overcome every challenge, emerging stronger and more in love than ever.

[Scene 5 - Comedy Strikes Again]

Dushyant attempting to fix a leaky faucet.

Dushyant: (holding a wrench) So, the leaks in our house decided to play hide and seek with me. But don't worry, folks, the wrench is mightier than the leak!

Mannat: (giggling) I married a handyman. Who knew fixing leaks could be so entertaining?

[Scene 6 - Surprises Unveiled]

Dushyant presenting a wrapped gift to Mannat.

Dushyant: (excitedly) Now, for the surprise of the day! Mannat, close your eyes.

Mannat closes her eyes as Dushyant reveals a beautifully framed picture of late Khwaaish.

Dushyant: (teary-eyed) Khwaaish will always be a part of our journey. Thank you, Noddy.

Mannat: (teary-eyed) Our past is woven into our present and future. Khwaaish, our eternal companion.

[Scene 7 - Baby Khwaaish's Debut]

Dushyant and Mannat holding a cradle, softly singing a lullaby.

Dushyant: (whispering) And introducing the newest member of our family - Baby Khwaaish. A bundle of joy, a piece of our hearts.

Mannat: (smiling) Our love multiplied, bringing a new chapter filled with baby giggles and endless love.

[Scene 8 - Furry Family Members]

Snow and Martha playing in the backyard.

Mannat: (pointing) Now, let's not forget our furry companions, Snow and Martha. They're not just pets; they're a part of our love story.

Dushyant: (petting Snow and Martha) True companions who've witnessed chapters of our journey.

[Scene 9 - Embracing Forever: A Family's Love Tale]

Dushyant, Mannat, Baby Khwaaish, Snow, and Martha sharing a sweet family hug.

Mannat: (smiling) Thanks for joining us on this incredible ride. Our journey has just begun, and we can't wait to share more love and laughter with all of you.

Dushyant: (looking at Mannat) Stay tuned for more adventures, surprises, and, of course, endless love. Our story continues, and it's a story we're writing together.

[Closing Scene]

Soft romantic music continues to play in the background as Mannat and Dushyant stand together, surrounded by the memories of their journey.

Mannat: (looking at Dushyant with a smile) Dushyant, before we close this beautiful chapter of our life, could you recite one of your cheesy poems? Just like the old days?

Dushyant: (grinning) Ah, you want a blast from the past, huh? (Clears throat)

In the pizza of love, you're my extra cheese,

A flavor so rich, it brings me to my knees.

Your smile, a topping, bright and divine,

Together we savor, in every cheesy line.

In the oven of romance, our hearts are baked,

A delicious concoction, love never faked.

With laughter as seasoning, sprinkled from above,

Our cheesy love story, a feast of joy and love.

So, let's share this pizza, hand in hand,

In the cheesy kingdom, forever we'll stand.

With each cheesy bite, our love will grow,

A delicious journey, just us in the dough!

Mannat: (laughing) Cheesy as ever, but it still melts my heart. Our love story, a blend of romance, laughter, and a touch of your cheesy poetry, is my favorite tale.

[Screen fades to black with a heartwarming quote: "Every love story is beautiful, but ours is my favorite."]

As Mannat and Dushyant watched their final video, they found themselves pleasantly surprised by the outcome—it had exceeded their expectations. The emotional depth, the artistic storytelling, and the genuine moments captured on camera left them in awe of what they had created. Overwhelmed with joy, they couldn't contain their excitement and quickly rushed to the Wishlist board. With triumphant smiles, they checked off another accomplishment, cheering and celebrating the fulfillment of yet another wish. In that moment of shared happiness, they marveled at how far they had come on their journey together.

(Above cheesy poem compares love to a pizza, with the person being addressed as the "extra cheese" that makes the love so rich and delightful. The verses playfully describe how their smiles and shared moments are like toppings on this romantic pizza, creating a delicious and joyful love story that they want to savor together. The poem encourages sharing the pizza of love hand in hand, symbolizing the enduring journey of their relationship.)

Wish #7- Creating their own Post-Wedding Video- Completed

Dushyant's inner thoughts echoed, realizing that only one wish remained on the Wishlist board—the last piece of their dreams puzzle. However, Mannat had silently placed her wish too, the aspiration to open a Cloud Kitchen. Accepting the responsibility, he geared up to fulfill not just his dream but hers too. Turning to Mannat with determination, he expressed, "Now it's time to bring your wish to life, Darling."

Mannat was pleasantly surprised, and in a playful tone, she handed him her cheque book, teasing, "Don't spend too much, okay? Focus on your dream, and I'll manage the rest. I can handle our family members well; you just go and live your dream now." Dushyant smiled at her support, realizing that they were not just life partners but dream custodians for each other.

In pursuit of his dream to open a Cloud Kitchen, Dushyant embarked on a comprehensive journey. He diligently scouted and secured a suitable location, then delved into the intricate process of setting up the kitchen. Every detail, from acquiring the necessary equipment to assembling a dedicated team of skilled laborers, required his focused attention.

The entire endeavor spanned a month, during which Dushyant poured his heart and soul into designing the perfect setup. The meticulous planning, the careful consideration of every aspect, and the customization of the menu to reflect his culinary vision all became crucial components of his new venture.

For Dushyant, this venture was not just about creating a business; it was a labor of love that held immense significance for his family. Understanding the weight of responsibility that rested on his shoulders, he put in long hours and invested not only his skills but also his passion. The kitchen setup became more than just a profession—it became a source of livelihood for his entire family, making every decision and effort he put into it even more vital.

This new venture symbolized not only the realization of his personal dream but also the creation of a sustainable source of income for his loved ones. Dushyant's dedication and hard work were driven by the profound understanding that the success of his Cloud Kitchen would directly impact the well-being and stability of his family, making it a venture of paramount importance in his life.

The day of the grand inauguration of Dushyant's Cloud Kitchen arrived, and it was not just an event; it was a celebration of dreams, hard work, and the love that had brought this culinary venture to life. As per tradition, a fire ritual was organized to seek the blessings of the divine for the prosperity and success of the business.

Mannat, filled with excitement, witnessed the kitchen for the first time. She couldn't help but marvel at the meticulous setup that Dushyant had passionately crafted. During the initial days of its formation, Mannat would express her eagerness to witness the kitchen in action. However, Dushyant, with a twinkle in his eye, insisted on saving the revelation for the grand inauguration day, a day he promised to share with his entire family.

As Mannat stepped into the kitchen, her eyes sparkled with pride and joy. This space, which was once a canvas of dreams and aspirations, had now materialized into a reality that stood before her. Her smile radiated the support and encouragement that had fueled Dushyant's journey.

In the kitchen, adorned with the auspicious glow of the fire ritual, Mannat surprised Dushyant with a beautifully framed picture of Khwaaish. It was a poignant reminder of the thread that bound them together, the source of their strength, and the silent witness to their journey. Dushyant, touched by this thoughtful gesture, carefully placed the photo on the kitchen wall, making it a part of the culinary haven he had created.

With the completion of the auspicious ritual and the warm blessings of their loved ones, the family, including Baby Khwaaish, Martha, Snow, and both sets of parents, left the kitchen to let the business breathe and come to life on its own.

In the quietude of the kitchen, Dushyant turned to Mannat, a mischievous glint in his eyes. "How about a date here, just the two of us? A celebration of the first day of our kitchen and our own little surprise."

Mannat, pleasantly surprised, agreed, "Okay, unexpected surprises are the best."

The kitchen buzzed with the soft hum of newly installed appliances and the tantalizing aroma of spices lingering in the air. Dushyant, adorned in his chef's hat, looked around with pride. Mannat stood at the entrance, her eyes sparkling with admiration.

Dushyant: (grinning) Well, what do you think, my love? Isn't it just perfect?

Mannat: (smiling) It's more than perfect, Noddy. I can feel the love and hard work you've put into this place.

Dushyant: (playfully) And you haven't even seen the best part yet. Follow me.

He led her to a beautifully set table in the corner of the kitchen. The flickering candles created a cozy ambiance, and a bouquet which he received on inauguration adorned the center.

Mannat: (surprised) A table for two in our own kitchen?

Dushyant: (winking) What can I say? I wanted our first date here to be unforgettable.

They took their seats, and Dushyant handed her a menu filled with delicacies from different cuisines.

Dushyant: (with a mischievous smile) Tonight, you're not just my wife; you're my special guest. Order anything your heart desires.

Mannat giggled and pretended to scan the menu seriously.

Mannat: (teasing) Hmm, I'll have the chef's special, please. Surprise me.

Dushyant chuckled and got to work, creating a culinary masterpiece with a dash of his signature humor. As Mannat observed him, she couldn't help but admire the passion he infused into every dish.

Dushyant: (presenting the dish) Voila! The chef's special – "Spaghetti Aglio e Olio with Roasted Vegetables" a dish made with love, laughter, and a pinch of Noddy magic.

Mannat: (impressed) You never fail to surprise me, Noddy.

They enjoyed their delightful meal, sharing laughter and stealing glances between bites. The kitchen, once filled with the clatter of pans and sizzling sounds, now echoed with the sweet symphony of their shared moments.

After a delightful dinner, Dushyant took Mannat by the hand and led her to a cozy corner in their kitchen. A soft glow illuminated the space as he revealed a surprise – his iPhone connected to a small screen, ready to showcase their journey.

Dushyant: (smiling) Ta-da! A little change of plans. Our very own impromptu setup for a trip down memory lane.

He tapped a few buttons on his iPhone, and the screen came alive with a slideshow of their cherished moments. The images flickered across the wall, creating a magical ambiance in their kitchen.

Mannat: (surprised) Oh, wow! This is amazing.

Dushyant: (chuckling) Well, you know, spontaneous plans are my specialty.

The images captured the essence of their relationship – from the first day they met in college to the goofy moments, the challenges they faced, and the joyous occasions, including the opening of their cloud kitchen.

Mannat: (smiling) It's like reliving our entire journey. Look at us, from being clueless college students to this moment – running our own kitchen.

Dushyant: (nostalgic) Time flies, doesn't it? But every moment led us here, and I wouldn't change a thing.

As the slideshow continued, soft music played in the background, adding a touch of romance to the atmosphere. The images transitioned seamlessly, and with each picture, their love story unfolded.

Mannat: (teary-eyed) You've made this so special, Noddy. I can't believe how far we've come.

Dushyant: (gentle smile) Our journey is far from over, Mannat. We have many more chapters to write.

The last slide displayed a message: "To be continued..."

Dushyant: (whispering) This is just the beginning, my love.

While they swayed in the dance, Mannat whispered softly in Dushyant's ear, her voice filled with a mix of excitement and tenderness.

Mannat: (whispering) You know, Noddy, our surprises always seem to align. I had a surprise too. We are going to be parents again. I'm pregnant with our baby, a little companion for Baby Khwaaish. I wanted to tell you during the inauguration, but you, always a step ahead, planned this spontaneous date. So, what do you say? Shall we embark on the journey of becoming parents for the second time?

Dushyant, in the midst of the dance, felt a rush of emotions. A radiant smile spread across his face, a perfect blend of surprise and overwhelming joy.

Dushyant: (whispering back) Mannat, you never cease to amaze me. This is incredible news! Our family is growing, and I couldn't be happier. Second time parents, here we come!

They continued to dance, wrapped in the warmth of the kitchen, surrounded by the love they had built together. The revelation added an extra layer of sweetness to their already memorable date, making it a moment they would cherish forever.

Mannat, with a playful smile, voiced her concern about her appearance changing during pregnancy.

Mannat: You know, Noddy, a few months down the line, I'll gain weight and might not look as attractive. I worry that your love might diminish.

Dushyant responded with a loving smile, reassuring her with his words. When you gain a little weight, and your belly swells with our child, it won't make you any less attractive. In fact, it'll be a beautiful sight. My responsibility to love you will only double. So, don't worry from my end.

Their laughter filled the kitchen, and Dushyant gently kissed Mannat, emphasizing his love for her regardless of any physical changes.

As they held each other, looking at Khwaaish's photo, Dushyant expressed the depth of their journey and the significance of the newfound wish.

Dushyant: This wish goes beyond the Wishlist, beyond the stars. It's a promise of more love, more laughter, and the joy of welcoming another member into our beautiful family.

Over the course of the next nine months, Dushyant transformed into Mannat's unwavering support system. He meticulously crafted a timetable, ensuring every need and whim of Mannat was catered to. From preparing timely meals to sweetly handling her mood swings, Dushyant embraced his role as a caring husband and an excited father-to-be.

As the days passed, Mannat found herself falling deeper in love with Dushyant. His commitment to their family, both present and future, was beyond anything she had imagined. She often expressed her gratitude to Dushyant, overwhelmed by his love and the beautiful moments they were sharing.

One evening, as they sat in the nursery they had prepared for the new member of their family, Mannat couldn't help but pour her heart out.

Mannat: Dushyant, you're not just an amazing husband and father, but you've become a beautiful soul in this form of a partner. These nine months have shown me that angels do exist, and they come in the form of pure souls like you.

Dushyant, a bit bewildered but with a warm smile, responded.

Dushyant: What are you talking about? I was going to say the same thing to you. Your quick decision at the adoption center changed my entire life. Now, after delivering our baby, I promise to take care of you and our family for the rest of my life.

Mannat, touched by his words, gently held his hand.

Mannat: I knew this; I trust you more than anyone else in this world, Noddy. Your love has made these nine months an unforgettable journey.

The pivotal day had finally arrived, a day entwined with the shared anticipation of labor pain and the thrill of awaiting the momentous news—Dushyant pacing nervously outside the delivery ward, akin to the restless nerves one experiences while waiting for crucial exam results. Meanwhile, Mannat, inside the ward, bore the physical intensity of labor pains, emblematic of the emotional tumult accompanying such significant life events.

The corridors echoed with a symphony of emotions as both sets of parents, cradling Baby Khwaaish in their laps, shared the collective anticipation. The atmosphere buzzed with an amalgamation of excitement, anxiety, and the profound joy of welcoming a new life.

As the clock ticked away, the doctor emerged from the delivery room, carrying news that would shape the destiny of their family.

Doctor: Congratulations! It's a boy.

Dushyant's face lit up with joy upon hearing the news. He rushed into the ward to be with Mannat. Seeing her lying on the bed, he couldn't contain his happiness. He gently kissed her forehead, expressing gratitude for completing their family.

Dushyant: Thank you, Mannat.

As Mannat lay there, exhausted yet elated, Dushyant held their baby boy for the first time. Tears of joy welled up in his eyes, and he whispered words of love to his newborn son.

Dushyant: You see, Baby Khwaaish, here's your younger brother.

Mannat joined in the moment, showering affection on their newborn. Laughter echoed through the room as they marveled at the newfound completeness of their family. A nurse, touched by the emotional scene, couldn't resist capturing the beautiful bond in a candid photograph.

This was more than a result; it was the culmination of their love story, the beginning of a new chapter filled with shared joys and responsibilities. The photograph, a snapshot of pure happiness, encapsulated the essence of their journey together.

The joyous arrival of new baby boy, filled Dushyant and Mannat's home with boundless happiness. Eager to celebrate this precious addition to their family, they decided to host a naming ceremony and welcome baby boy into their lives officially.

The day of the ritual arrived, and their home was adorned with vibrant decorations, symbolizing the joy that baby boy brought with him. Close friends and family gathered for the auspicious occasion, ready to share in the laughter and love that permeated the air.

Dushyant, donning a quirky apron that read "Dad in Charge," took charge of the festivities with his unique blend of comedy and charm. Mannat, looking radiant and content, held baby boy close, with Baby Khwaaish, Snow, and Martha adding their own brand of joyful chaos to the celebration.

The naming ceremony unfolded with traditional rituals, blessings, and heartfelt moments. As the priest announced the name "Nitaaksh," meaning "Gift of God," a collective cheer filled the room. Dushyant and Mannat exchanged smiles, knowing that their family was now complete with the arrival of their little Nitaaksh.

With the rituals completed, the atmosphere transformed into a lively after-birth party. Laughter echoed as friends and family engaged in cheerful banter. Dushyant, the self-proclaimed chef of the day, showcased his culinary skills, attempting to balance an array of dishes while entertaining everyone with his humorous commentary.

Mannat, the gracious hostess, moved effortlessly through the crowd, ensuring that everyone felt the warmth of their hospitality. Baby Khwaaish, full of excitement, proudly showed off the newest member of the family to their guests, adding an extra layer of joy to the celebration.

The party continued with games, anecdotes, and shared stories of parenthood. Dushyant, always the entertainer, initiated a series of light-hearted competitions, from baby bottle chugging contests to diaper-changing races, creating an atmosphere filled with laughter and camaraderie.

As the evening unfolded, the laughter and joy became the melody of the celebration. The after-birth party became a beautiful tapestry of shared happiness, where the love for Nitaaksh and the joy of togetherness bound everyone in a delightful embrace.

The night concluded with heartfelt goodbyes and promises to meet again soon. Dushyant and Mannat stood at the threshold of their home, surrounded by the warmth of their loved ones, grateful for the abundance of love that filled their lives. The after-birth party became a cherished chapter in their book of life, a vibrant page that reflected the exuberance of family, friendship, and the endless joys of parenthood.

Under the canvas of the evening sky, adorned with a myriad of stars, Dushyant and Mannat found themselves immersed in a poignant moment of reflection. The celestial expanse seemed to echo with the laughter, tears, and love that had woven the tapestry of their extraordinary journey.

As they looked up, both Dushyant and Mannat felt an overwhelming sense of gratitude. In the quiet beauty of that moment, they remembered Khwaaish—the choreographer of their love story, the angel who had scripted their destinies from above. The wishes on the board were not merely whims but cosmic dreams, wishes that had gone beyond the stars.

Dushyant, with a heart full of emotions, turned to Mannat. "These were not just wish lists, Mannat. They were Wishlist beyond the stars, cosmic whispers that Khwaaish brought into our lives. She will forever remain alive in our hearts."

Mannat, her eyes reflecting the vastness of the universe, smiled through a cascade of emotions. "Our baby Khwaaish is the incarnation of her wishes and her, a living testament to the love that transcends dimensions."

Dushyant gently took Mannat's hand, and under the celestial canopy, they spoke words that resonated with the depth of their connection. "I've met many angels in my life—the first was Khwaaish, my first love; the second is you, Mannat, the love of my life; and the last but not least, our Baby Khwaaish, a radiant incarnation of all our wishes."

As they stood beneath the cosmic tapestry, the echoes of laughter, the warmth of shared tears, and the enduring love formed a symphony that would linger in their hearts forever. Khwaaish, the unseen writer of their tale, had choreographed a story that transcended the ordinary, leaving behind a legacy of love, resilience, and the eternal dance of wishes that reached beyond the stars.

In that concluding moment, as Dushyant and Mannat embraced the beauty of their shared journey, they silently thanked the real angel who had once graced their lives and now watched over them from the celestial realms. The story had ended, but its echoes would resonate through time—a timeless melody of love, laughter, and wishes that soared beyond the stars, creating a legacy that would be remembered for ages to come. Thankyou Khwaaish!

The story isn't over yet, my friends. The last wish has also been fulfilled by documenting their life journey i.e., "Write a book on their life". Every wish from the Wishlist has been checked off, and their tale has been beautifully penned. This book is an evidence.

All wishes from Wishlist Borad Fulfilled-

Wish #1- A gift to each other that is both Expensive and cheaper at the same time- Manifested

Wish #2- Five Weekend Dates without Phones- Manifested

Wish #3- Wish to have a First child as a girl- Manifested

Wish #4- Switching each other houses and make Dinner for a Family - Manifested

Wish #5- Taking the Girl's Surname after Marriage- Manifested

Wish #6- Propose in a Unique way for Marriage- Manifested

Wish #7- Creating their own Post-Wedding Video- Manifested

Wish #8- Own a Dream House- Manifested

Wish #9- Having a Cat and Dog as Pets. - Manifested

Wish #10- Name A Star Together- Manifested

Wish #11- Write a Book on their life- Manifested

Wish #12- Added on Mannat request- Opening a Cloud Kitchen- Manifested

Let's End this book with a beautiful poem:

In the hands of fate, some things elude our grasp,

Like life and death, within destiny's clasp.

But how to live, that's a choice we wield,

Live today, forget yesterday's field.

Create goodness today, tomorrow unfolds,

As long as intentions are pure, the universe holds.

In any relationship, share love without a cost,

The universe multiplies, love is never lost.

Patience and hope, don't undervalue their might,

In their quiet strength, a powerful light.

In the cosmic dance, Khwaaish played her part,

Fulfilling wishes, eternally engraved in heart.

Life's lessons from this tale, open your heart wide,

Live freely, smile broadly, in every stride.

Miracles happen, anytime, anywhere,

This story teaches, live without a care.

Khwaaish's tale, a lesson so bright,

Strong will paves paths, trust your inner light.

In her gaze, a truth revealed,

Willpower conquers, the Universe yields.

Wishlist beyond the stars, the book's name,

Reflecting the miracles, life's cosmic game.

(This poem reflects on the interplay between fate and personal choices. It acknowledges that certain aspects of life are beyond our control, like life and death, but emphasizes the power of choosing how to live in the present. The verses encourage creating goodness today with pure intentions, sharing love without expectations, and recognizing the strength in patience and hope. The cosmic dance symbolizes the interconnectedness of individuals with the universe. The poem teaches life lessons of embracing openness, living with a smile, and being receptive to miracles at any moment. Khwaaish's tale teaches: with strong will, paths unfold, trust your inner light, and the Universe's secrets are told. The title, "Wishlist beyond the stars," suggests that life's miracles and lessons extend beyond the ordinary, reflecting a cosmic perspective on existence.)

Acknowledgment

Writing a book is a journey that involves the contributions and support of numerous individuals who enrich the process. I extend my heartfelt gratitude to everyone who played a role in bringing this work to fruition.

Special Acknowledgment to a Special person:

My heartfelt thanks to the silent force that kindled the flame of my writing journey. Dear special person, your impact resonates in every word penned on these pages. You are my Guardian Angel, steering me towards this creativity with your unseen hand. This book is a tribute to your influence, a silent muse who deserves recognition, though unnamed. Grateful for your guiding light and Keep Inspiring.

With heartfelt appreciation!

Publishing Team:

A sincere expression of gratitude to the dedicated publishing team whose expertise and diligence transformed my words into this tangible reality. Your commitment to excellence and unwavering support have been instrumental in bringing this book to life. Thank you for your tireless efforts and belief in the power of storytelling.

Readers:

To the readers who will embark on this adventure, your interest and curiosity are the fuel that drives the narrative forward. I hope the words within these pages resonate with you and provide moments of reflection, inspiration, and joy. Books are a collective creation, and I am honored to contribute to the world of literature.

Thank you, each of you, for being indispensable contributors to this profound journey. Looking forward to feedback.

(Abhay Chaudhary)